JONATHAN CREED

A
SUTHERLAND
MURDER

PAUL PUBLISHING

First published in Great Britain in 2020 by

Paul Publishing Ltd

1 3 5 7 9 10 8 6 4 2

ISBN (Paperback) 978-1-8383331-0-2

ISBN (e-book) 978-1-8383331-1-9

Typeset and Printed in UK by
A4 Design & Print Ltd, 50 Seafield Road, Inverness, Highland, Scotland IV1 1SG

A SUTHERLAND MURDER

JONATHAN CREED

PROLOGUE

East Sutherland 1954

The hired car drove cautiously out of Dornoch, the driver, was going at a very slow 25 miles per hour. Her husband looked across to her and then in the rear mirror to his son, Bill, seated on the rear seat engrossed in a 'Dandy Summer Special'. They had come by train to Dornoch from Inverness. First having to change at a place called 'The Mound' before taking a light train to Dornoch. Here they had arranged to hire a car for the rest of the holiday. Now they were driving northwards.

Half an hour later, Bill had finished the comic and was looking out of the car window as they waited at the level crossing for the train to return to Inverness. His Father looked across to his wife.

"Think we had better find somewhere to stop soon." She glanced at the AA map on her lap, and following the road with her finger, pointed to a small village.

"We could stop here, at Golspie, it's about 4 miles further on, and looks interesting, there is a castle to the north and appears to have a bit of a built-up area on the main road."

The level crossing gates swung back, and they drove on towards Golspie. As she had thought, the place had quite a few shops along the main road, while small roads led off to the left. The sea lapped gently on the right of the road. They stopped in a small car park and got out and walked the length of the village to purchase the items needed for a picnic. The Husband got some money from a bank, before driving on to a small historical mound, called Carn Liath Broch, around three miles north of Golspie. The car park was on the opposite side of the road. They walked over to where the Broch was. Bill ran on ahead following the Carn around in its circular style, he made his way to the top. Looking down at his parents now setting out the picnic things. He ran down to join them..

After the picnic was finished and cleared away, Bill walked back up the Broch to the top of the walls. Once there he looked down into the centre. Two men could be seen fighting. One grabbed the other and pushed him to the ground. There was a flash in the sunlight, then the man on the ground appeared not to move. The other man, bent down and took something from the other man's pocket before running towards the car park. Bill stood, still taking in what he had just seen, then raced back towards his parents to tell them.

"I've just seen a man knocked down and robbed."

"Nonsense, that sort of thing doesn't happen up here." said his Father.

"You've been reading to many books" added his Mother.

"I tell you I've just seen a man knocked down and robbed. Come and see if you don't believe me."

"Ok, but it had better be the truth." His father added as he got to his feet and followed Bill back up and into the centre to where he had seen the two men. There was nobody there. A small red stain, hardly noticeable by anybody, was on the grass, but no other sign of either of the two men. Bill ran on ahead, and looked around, only their car was in the car park, and the road was empty of any vehicles.

"Two men fighting, ha, you read too much, and it was in your imagination Bill." I'm going back to rest; you carry on playing. "His father left him and walked down to the picnic and stretched out on the ground to promptly fall asleep. Bill thought to himself, he's wrong, I did see the men there fighting…

Chapter 1

Oxford in May 1960 was a bustling place. Students going to and from their exams. They didn't take any notice of the tourists trying to walk up or down 'The High' the main street in Oxford. Queens college front was particularly busy. The buses stopped there and being opposite the examination schools, students spilled out onto the road. Ronald Burgess waited quietly. He had his back to the college looking as though he was a tourist. Taking care to blend in, not wanting to be noticed by anybody. Ronald had plans for at least one, if not two of the students. He saw a young man waiting with a bottle of champagne. Obviously a student but waiting for his girlfriend, Ronald thought to himself. The ideal target. He moved a bit closer. The girl appeared at the bottom of the examination schools steps. A small strap of her handbag was looped around her shoulder. She looked around as though looking for somebody. The man gave a wave, then surged forward with the crowd of other students across the road towards the girl. He waved and yelled her name but in the noise of the traffic nobody couldn't hear what it was. The girl must have though. she looked towards the man and ran to meet him. Ronald followed the two of them. He took out his sharp knife, and as he approached the pair, slipped by and cut the strap with one hand while taking the handbag in the other, she hadn't noticed anything at all. He moved away towards the river and the Eastgate Hotel. Ronald planned to get off The High as soon as possible in order to see what he had got this time.

+

Bertie Parker, one of the University Proctors, had seen Ronald take the bag, but had been unable to do anything about it, as there were just too many students between him and the thief. He thought he recognised the man but wasn't too sure. Had he recognised him, then he might be attached to the University in some way, but why would a man risk a good job just to steal a handbag, it made no sense to him. He had noted that the man had gone towards the Eastgate hotel He may just catch the thief. Bertie turned and went back inside to use a route through the examination schools into Merton Street.

+

In Merton Street Ronald stopped in the shadow of Merton College and opened the bag, it was a good leather one, inside he found the usual items that he had expected. The purse attracted his attention, unlike most ladies purses, this one was bulging with twenty pound notes. He took a quick count of it, two thousand pounds. It was too much he had expected about a hundred, this was enough to get a small house. Why would a student, be carrying that sort of money in an exam? Quickly he put the purse back in the bag, and walked quickly into the entrance of the college, the porter in reception called out to him.

"Mr Burgess, there is some post for you." He nodded his head towards the pigeonholes, Ronald moved over to the one with his name on it, took it and after thanking the man, walked up to his rooms.

+

Bertie opened the door onto Merton Street just in time to see the thief walk into Merton College. So, he thought to himself, is this where he is based? He walked over to the reception desk and asked the porter who had just come in?

"That'll be Mr Burgess, one of the Lecturers, teaches Botany if I recall correctly. He started working here, if you can call it working, last year."

"Thank you, that is most helpful."

"Do you want me to tell him you called?"

"No, that is not necessary, thank you." Bertie turned and walked back the way he had come, while thinking to himself about what he had just witnessed.

+

Ronald shut the door to his room. He was shaking, while he liked to take small occasional risks, and had planned this, he hadn't expected there to be that much money. Most students wouldn't bother the police over a small amount would they? But this would be different, nobody would stay quiet over a robbery of that much money he thought to himself. He walked over to the side and poured himself a large whisky, drinking it in one gulp, he poured another, and then stopped himself, this had to be thought through carefully, and where should he put the money for now, he wondered? Then he thought about the wretched handbag, he needed to get rid of it, and quickly too. He took it off the bed, where he had thrown it when he came into the room, took the money out, and took a little more time to check its contents again. At the bottom of the bag was a small plastic bag of purple pills. Maybe the student wouldn't go to the police after all. He put the contents into a paper bag. Then placed it into the handbag and slide it under the bed. That would have to do for the moment, till night came and he had a chance to get rid of it somewhere unseen.

+

Bertie, having walked back to the Examination Schools, went home thinking maybe he could turn this information into something a bit more lucrative for himself. At his dinner table that evening, he put together a small typed note addressed to Mr R Burgess.

Very early the following morning, Bertie cycled down to Merton College. Once at the college, he padlocked it and entered the main entrance. Nobody in the lodge, so he moved to the rack of pigeon- holes on the wall and placed the envelope in the marked 'BURGESS" before leaving. He cycled to Christchurch College. He knew one of the porters there and had previously arranged to leave his bike in his safe keeping.

Meantime, Ronald was at Folly Bridge, dropping the handbag into the river. He had got rid of the contents by dropping them one at a time in different rubbish bins on his way. Leaving the bag open water poured in and it quickly disappeared into the depths. Satisfied with the result, he turned and briskly started to walk back to Merton College.

Twenty minutes later, he was at the main entrance and glancing over to the pigeon-holes as was his habit, was surprised to see an envelope in his. He took it and a quick glance revealed it had not been posted, but hand delivered. He turned to the porter in charge,

"Did you put this here?"

"No sir, the main post hasn't been yet, I only started about half an hour ago, and it was there then. Maybe somebody left in there last night. Do you want me to ask the other porter sir?"

"No thanks." Ronald turned and walked up to his room. Once inside he sat at his desk and taking up a paperknife, carefully slit the top of the envelope. He took out a piece of folded blue notepaper, he opened it, and saw that it had been typed. Quickly, he read the message..

```
'I saw what you did, and know that you would not
want a fuss or to risk your job would you? Now,
should I do the right thing and tell the authori-
```

```
ties about this, or….'
```
"Damn!" Ronald said out loud. How did anybody know who he was or where he was based? He must have been followed, and with the names on the pigeonholes, it would be easy to find his and put a note in there for him to find. He looked again at the note, no address he noted wryly to himself. Well, he would just have wait and see. In the meantime, he needed to find a safe place for the cash that he had stolen. He wondered why things always keep happening to him, not thinking for one moment that he had brought this upon himself.

CHAPTER 2

Bertie, having dropped the note off, made his way to the examination schools, in order to help get it ready for that days exams. The desks had been arranged weeks ago. Now it was just a question of checking to see that there were any notes or papers stuck to the underside of the desks, as had happened in the past. He picked up the keys to the Halls and made his way up the stairs. His day was going well, he thought to himself, and wondered what Mr Burgess was thinking about his note.

+

Ronald was certainly not having a good day, although as it was exam week. His lectures were finished for the year. However, he still needed to be around in case of any queries that might arise, when the exam paper was read by the students for the first time. All day he wondered was who was behind the note.

+

Bertie had noticed Burgess, with a tired and weary face, enter the building that morning. He had followed, as a member of staff, he was not likely to draw any attention to himself. He wondered what he should put in the next note, a time and place to meet perhaps? No, that could come later, a suggestion of an amount. He moved away to a near office, looked up and down the corridor, then unlocked the door, and entered. A typewriter was on the desk. Bertie sat down, then taking out a piece of paper from the shelf in front of the desk, started to type..

Half an hour later he left the office, and relocked it, Bertie took time to check that Burgess was still in the examination hall, he didn't think that he wouldn't be, but best to check first, he thought to himself. Having satisfied himself that Burgess wouldn't be out of the hall for some time, he went down the stairs and out of the building and crossed over to Queens lane. At the pillar box there he posted the new note to Burgess. Satisfied that nobody had seen him, he walked briskly back to the Examination halls to continue his days' work..

+

For the last time that day Burgess stole a glance at his watch, two minutes to go. He watched the large clock with its second hand sweeping around it, as the seconds ticked down. "One minute to go" he called out, the students didn't move, or acknowledge, they were already checking or making last minute alterations, a few had already left, either brilliant or knew that they would fail anyhow and didn't see the point to staying in a dusty hall for a few hours. "Times up. Put down your pens and wait for the papers to be collected, do not talk until this has been completed." The same ritual would go on year after year he thought to himself. Ten minutes later, the hall was emptying, as students left, some quietly talking to friends, others silent and quiet. The exam papers had been gathered and bundled together, the invigilators had packed up and left, Ronald too, had left the hall, and made his way back to Merton, though this time he kept looking behind himself to see if he was being followed..

..Later in his room Ronald sat at his desk, his head in his hands, why was there no note? He was so sure that there would have been a follow up one, or was the first one just a student prank? He got up and walked towards the door of his rooms. He would go out for a walk and stretch his legs for a bit. Maybe that would help him decide what to do.

+

Bertie had collected his bike and ridden to his home in Headington. Having eaten his tea, he decided he would go for a cycle ride. He smiled to himself as he thought of what Mr Burgess would be going through, probably panicking as to why no note had arrived. Well he would soon see what would develop.

CHAPTER 3

The following day Ronald paced his room while glancing at his watch. He had found out that the post was sorted by 10.00am As soon as it was 9.50 he made his way down the lobby. He glanced at his box. Shaking his head in disbelief, he checked it but there was nothing there. He went out and walked through to Christchurch Meadow and down to the river. Was it a hoax, he wondered to himself, something a student had done as a prank? Fishing in his pocket, he took out the original note, now folded and creased from being in his pocket, and re-read it for the umpteenth time..

'I saw what you did, and know that you would not want a fuss or to risk your job would you? Now, should I do the right thing and tell the authorities about this, or....'

...Maybe he had jumped to conclusions, there was nothing to link this to the theft was there?

+

Bertie was having a nice day off, there would be no more exams till next week, and he sat on a park bench in the sunshine, overlooking the library, wondering what Mr Burgess would make of his latest note.

+

Ronald walked up The High towards the examination schools, he had crossed over, and gone to buy a newspaper, but became distracted by the sight of fire engines and police at Queens College. Forgetting about his newspaper, he walked towards Queens and the fire engines. As he approached, he could see hoses on the ground going up Queens lane, a fireman stopped him going any closer.

"Can't let you get too close; please can you go back and cross over the other side."

"Yes ok, but first can you tell me what is going on please?"

"A fire was started on some rubbish, which was stacked near the post box, we've put the fire out, but are having the mail checked to see if any of it is salvageable, the fire was pretty intense, and the red paint has been completely destroyed. Now if you don't mind?" He indicated to Ronald to cross over the road, and then he started to stop the next person trying to get through. Ronald crossed over and walked up to the Covered Market to get out of the heat. The avenues of shops and stalls seemed to slow the pace of the fast moving 1960's and he walked up and down the avenues, looking at fruit and veg, then cheeses and the ripe smell of a mix of all things being sold hung heavily in the air. The sunlight came in through windows, high on the roof, but it was never as hot as outside. He purchased some fruit and left via Market Street before going to Cornmarket.

+

Bertie had gone home and was waiting for the first edition of the Oxford Mail to be delivered. While he knew that the paperboy usually delivered the later editions, he liked to keep up to date. He had an arrangement with the owner of the corner shop to have the first edition of the paper dropped off. The noise of the letterbox brought him to his feet. He walked down the hall and picked up the paper. He took it into the front room where sunlight was coming in through the windows. Sitting down in his favourite chair, he unfolded it, and stared at the headline. 'POSTBOX FIRE STOPS POST' he read the article, as usual the headline was just a catcher for attention. The fire had started with a pile of rubbish that happened to be next to the postbox. He almost didn't bother reading all of it, till the words, 'Queens College closed for short while' jumped out at him. Then re-reading the piece, he saw it was the same postbox that he had used. He wondered if the box had been emptied before the fire, or was it his bad luck that the note might have been destroyed? He would wait and see what Ronald thought of the latest note, or maybe he would have to write another one for Ronald.

+

The next day, sitting in the pigeonholes, was a large brown envelope addressed to R.BURGESS, MERTON COLLEGE, OXFORD. It had a sticker on the envelope: We are sorry the contents got damaged in our care, please do check inside, if anything is missing phone the number below:

Ronald was on the point of walking through the doors of Merton, when the porter called him over.

"Piece of post for you Mr Burgess. One of the letters damaged in the fire, I fancy. They asked if you can check it is intact and let them know if anything is missing."

"Thank you, I'll do that." Ronald went and collected his post, and walked out to Merton St, opening the envelope as he did so. Inside was another envelope, smaller, but along one edge it was burnt. The end had been cut open; this could also mean that somebody else had read the contents. Damn! He took a seat on a nearby bench and read the note in full..

> "By now, you will probably be wondering what I saw. I can tell you what that was in due course, but in order that I know you will agree to my ~~suggestion~~ or demand, that you do not go to the police, I want you to go to the top of Carfax Tower and wait for more instructions. I'll let you know the time and day next time."

Ronald noted that one word was crossed through and two words repeated. It told him that this was a person who didn't have much money, or they would have made a clean copy, and probably re-read it as well. He wondered when the next note may arrive. He got up and started walking briskly towards the Botanical Gardens.

CHAPTER 4

Two days later, the third note had come that morning, and it was very different to the others.

```
    Good morning Mr Burgess, have you had time to
think about the last letter? Maybe you didn't get
it, so here it is again.
    By now, you will probably be wondering what I
saw, I can tell you that was the theft. I know you
will agree to my request or demand, that you do
not go to the police, but go instead to the top of
Carfaz Tower on and wait for more instructions.
I'll let you know the time and day within a day or
so." It wasn't the same, nearly, but not quite.
The repeating of the phrase and the crossing out
had gone, but Carfax had been made into Cardfaz,
maybe this person didn't usually type, the X and Z
were next to each other. He would just have to
wait. Then he thought to himself, why was he think-
ing he didn't get the previous letter? The only
thing that he could think of, of any significance
was the fire near the postbox, maybe the note
writer, lived or worked nearby?
```
Bertie sat in his front room, arms folded and half asleep. He didn't have a lot of money and had been wondering how much to ask Mr Burgess for before dozing off. He awoke to the smell of burning, getting up quickly, he made his way to the kitchen, where smoke was coming under the door. He flung the door open and a whoosh of flame came towards him, he cried out in pain, and fell to the floor unconscious.

+

The Policeman stood looking at the half burnt out house. The neighbours of the adjoining house had been evacuated, as the property had yet to be checked for structural safety. He had got here first and had dragged the body out of the burning building. On finding out the person was still alive, had called it in and an ambulance had taken the man to the Radcliffe Infirmary. That was three days ago, and the man was still unconscious and unable to say anything.

+

Ronald had started to relax, he hadn't heard anything further, and was thinking that it was some sort of student prank. Just happened to be a good guess writing about 'the theft' he wryly thought to himself. He was on his way to the University of Oxford Local Examination Offices in North Oxford, there was a query over one or two students papers, he had been asked to attend a meeting of like minds to grade the marks in question.

+

The nurse looked at the man lying in the bed, his face and hands badly burnt, it was a blessing that he was still unconscious she thought to herself. Her hand moved towards the instruments and noted the readings on her clipboard, then hung it on the bottom of the bed. She left the room and walked down the corridor, her shoes clicking on the floor as she went.

+

Ronald leaned back in his chair and stifled a yawn, it had been a long day, he thought to himself. If there was nothing in his box tonight, he would put the whole thing down as a student prank. But he would not be risking anything similar for a long time to come, it was too risky, too much to lose. He smiled as the meeting broke up, and the team went their separate ways. He walked out and down the road to a nearby bus stop to wait for the next bus to the centre. Ronald got off the bus in Cornmarket, busy as usual, the mix of students, visitors and workers all trying to get off or on buses. He made his way to the stockbrokers in Turl Street, to finalise the order of purchasing some stock that he decided to use the stolen money for. It had occurred to him that a bank would be too nosey as to where it had come from, where a Stockbroker, just took it and the order for the stock, no questions asked. Rather than taking it all at once, he had spread it over 3 days, a bit each day. Nobody enquired as to where it had come from. Ronald had left very clear instructions that any dividends were to be reinvested in more stock. That way, no paperwork for any nosey cleaner or anybody else to find. He also told them that he would collect the statements every six months. He didn't plan to keep any paperwork that was sent, just read the current value and then burn it.

CHAPTER 5

Headington Oxford 1965 Springtime.

Bertie awoke and as was his habit, touched his face lightly. Few people had the chance to change the way they looked, and he had taken the opportunity when it was offered to him after his accident in the fire all those years ago. It had been a shock to find his home nearly destroyed, but he had had insurance, and that paid for the rebuild and the University had been very understanding about him having to give up the job they had arranged a small pension as well. He got out of bed and set about his usual daily routine. Shave, wash, and breakfast, then collect his paper and walk in the park, do some shopping, in the fishmongers today, as it was Friday and then back to the house. It was a dreary existence, but he knew he couldn't afford anything else. He would have liked a holiday, but that too was out of the question.

At the same time, Ronald was up and out walking through Old Headington. He had moved there three years ago, his initial investment in the stock market had been a winner, by some fluke of chance, he had, it appeared, bought low and seen the price of stock rise through the roof. On the advice of the stockbroker, he had sold about a third and bought a small house in Old Headington. He could afford it, his job paid well, and he was relaxed about life in general. He had decided that morning that he would go on holiday, nowhere too exotic, perhaps Devon and Cornwall, or maybe Wales Ronald thought to himself as he walked through the dappled lit trees that lined the road on each side.

+

A few hours later, Ronald was to be found at the Coop Furniture store, choosing some new chairs for his office at home. Headington had such a good range of shops, okay most of it was owned by the Co-op on that side of the London Road, but the variety of independent shops made it a very nice place to live. Pleased with his choice of chairs and having paid for them and arranged for delivery that afternoon, he walked out into the sunlight. He stood for a few minutes on the pavement wondering if fish would make a change for today, deciding it would, he crossed the road.

Bertie, now walking briskly towards the fishmonger, got there just a few minutes after Ronald had just entered. To start with, he took no notice of any of the other customers, then he glanced up, and then took a second look, wasn't that man who stole the handbag off the student, how long ago? A long time, he had quite forgotten about that whole part of his previous life. Quickly he gave his order, and paid for the fish, then left, and stepping back into the shade of the roller blind that was stretched out in front of a cycle shop, he watched the man, leave the shop and walk towards Barclays Bank, on the corner of Old High St and London Road. On the spur of the moment, Bertie decided to follow him and perhaps learn where he might be working now…

…Twenty minutes later saw Ronald walk up the short path to his front door. Bertie who was a short distance behind, noted the house that he entered. Then Bertie turned back excitedly towards his own house. Maybe, just maybe, he might have that holiday he promised himself sooner than he had planned.

+

That evening Bertie was the most active he had been since his accident, after his meal. He cleared up and then took out his typewriter, something he had bought when he had refurnished the home. Purchased from the local second -hand shop, and just had needed a good clean and a new ribbon, but since he had not much to do, he had cleaned it up and then lost interest in it but now he had a use for it. Taking a clean piece of paper, he carefully inserted it between the rollers and after making sure it was square, started to type..

You thought you had got away with it, didn't you? Well, you may have done for a few years ok? Now I am asking for payment for my silence to be continued.. I would want the money in cash, notes of £1 and £5 and I'll tell you where to leave it in the next note..

Satisfied, he removed it and carefully folded it lengthwise and then corner to corner and placed it in a small envelope. He had remembered the man's name but didn't put that on the envelope. He just sealed it, and then stood up and walked to get his coat and picking up the note, left the house, and briskly walked towards the house he had seen Ronald enter.

+

Ronald sat in his lounge sipping a Scottish whisky. The fire crackled in the grate, and all was peaceful and right with the world. The letterbox rattled and whatever had been put through, landed on the mat. Rising slowly, he made his way towards the front door. On the floor was, face down, a brown envelope. Curious now, he stooped down and picked it up. Funny, he thought to himself, no name or address. Maybe everybody was getting one. Ronald walked back to his lounge, sat down and opened it, he took out the folded note, and unfolded it and then read, and re-read it.

```
    'You thought you had got away with it, didn't
you? Well, you may have done for a few years, but
now I am asking for payment for my silence to be
continued.. I would want the money in cash, notes
of £1 and £5 and I'll tell you where to leave it
in the next note..'
```

Ronald gave a small groan, after all these years and he foolishly had thought it was a student prank, but of course it wasn't. He quickly finished his drink and went and poured a large replacement. Getting the cash wasn't a problem. Would the demands stop there he wondered? Why now after so long, how long? Six, no five, years. He couldn't do anything but sit tight and wait for the next letter. Wait, though, he could get some cash tomorrow, it would be handy to have some ready in the house anyway. Then he remembered that today was Friday, and the banks would be closed. Well he would just have to sit it out then..

Bertie had stood for a while outside the house. He wondered what made a man like become a thief? Then he walked back to his home, where the typewriter sat, as though a faithful dog waiting for his next task. Bertie sighed, and sat down and decided to type a few of the messages together.

Two hours and a lot of corrected mistakes later, he had finished and beside him sat a small pile of 4 envelopes. He had remembered to type the envelopes this time, and each one was just typed with an R.B. on the front.

CHAPTER 6

Saturday morning saw Ronald rise early, he hadn't slept well, and when he came down, lying on the floor was the post. He gathered it up, and saw, besides the usual bills, an envelope with just R.B. on the outside. He rapidly opened it, dropping the others on the floor in his haste, and ran his eyes over the message.

```
    I don't want too much money, but enough that
will give me a holiday. A nice holiday in Whales,
that would be sufficient recompenses for my si-
lence. Used notes one and five pounds. Two Hundred
and fifty should be enough. The next message will
say how to pay…
```

Ronald scratched his head. The amount wasn't a problem, but was it an opportunist he wondered. Still, he would get the money, and that would be the end of the matter. Wouldn't be able to buy the nice car he had had his eyes on, but would live in peace, without any worries. He walked through to the kitchen and started to make breakfast.

+

Bertie was pleased with himself, he had, he thought, got the man probably a bit scared, well serve him right. A nice holiday in Scotland, that would be his plan, nowhere near Wales. He would get a copy of Exchange and Mart today and see if anywhere was available. Not to book, but to check and enquire. Now, lunchtime, would be a good time to drop the next note.

+

Ronald had decided not to go for his usual walk that morning, but instead had been looking at his bank statements, he had enough cash in one account, he was pleased to discover, so on Monday would pay the bank a visit, and take out three hundred pounds. He heard the door letterbox click and almost ran to pick up the envelope on the floor. He opened it, thinking to himself, this man is for real, no delay this time. His eyes read the note. Short and to the point the note read:-

```
    OK. ON MONDAY, PUT THE TWO HUNDRED AND FIFTY
POUNDS IN A CLOTH MONEY BAG, NOTES TO BE USED AND
```

IN BUNDLES OF FIFTY POUNDS. THE BAG IS TO BE LEFT
IN THE PARK BY THE LIBRARY UNDER THE METAL STEPS.
NO POLICE, NO HANGING AROUND. LEAVE IT AT 12.00NOON
AND THEN LEAVE YOURSELF.
  DON'T TRY TO SPOT ME. ANY FUNNY BUSINESS, AND
I'LL GO STRAIGT TO MERTON COLLEGE AND THE POLICE.

Ronald thought to himself, this was the real thing, he would do as he was told and then it would be all over.

+

Monday morning at 9.30 saw Ronald waiting patiently at the bank for it to open. When it did, he made his way inside and over to one of the three counters. The young lady looked up at him.

"Yes Sir, how can I help you today?"

"I want to make a cash withdrawal please, for three hundred pounds."

"That's a lot of money, more than I have in the drawer, I'll have to check, do you mind waiting?"

"No, here is my cheque, you can see it is drawn on this branch." He handed the cheque through and she took it and rose and moved to the back of the room, where two men sat. A short discussion followed, then she returned to the counter.

"That's perfectly in order, it will be here shortly, how do you want the money?"

"Five and One pound notes. It's for a holiday." He added, to give some credibility to drawing out such a large amount.

"Somewhere nice?"

"Wales." He replied, the place popping into his head. Why had he said anywhere at all, he thought silently to himself.

"Very nice, I haven't been there myself, but am told it is nice. Here you are Sir." She quickly counted the money down in front of him and then bundled it together.

"Do you think I might have a bank bag to carry it in please?"

"No problem, here you are," She stooped down, and picked up a white bag, into which she dropped the money. "Anything else Sir?"

"Not today, thank you." Ronald rose and left the bank clutching the bag of money to his chest. He went home and after locking the front door, emptied the bag. He counted the money asked for into bundles as requested. Shortly before twelve, he left his house and walked briskly to the library in the park. He got there a minute or so before twelve, and stuffed the bag under the steps, then taking a quick look around, nobody in sight, left it and walked towards the exit.

Bertie had been watching most of this from the top of the park by the bowling green and had nodded to himself with a grin as he saw a man approach and leave a bag where he had been asked to leave it. Bertie hurried down towards the library, a few people were leaving, but didn't pay any attention to him, as he sat on the bench between the two stairs going to the main entrance. When nobody was about, he stood up, walked the two or three steps and took the bag. He dropped it into a cloth bag of his own and walked slowly out of the park. If the police had been informed, this would be the moment that they would swoop, but nothing happened. Bertie walked openly out of the park and home. Once at home he tipped the bag out onto the dinner table, and sat mesmerised, by the bundles of money, deciding he needed a rare drink, he got a small sherry, and toasting the money, murmured, "To all foolish thieves and robbers" then tipped the glass back.

+

Ronald sat that afternoon in his house, he had done what was asked, and there had been no further notes. Sighing, he decided to go for a walk, a long walk, perhaps down to Oxford, the back way, it would make a change. Getting out of the house, he set off, at a pace that would have impressed a Guardsman, and forgot all of his problems.

+

Bertie, having counted and recounted all the money, decided to drop the last note he had written, a sarcastic 'thank you', through Ronald's letterbox. He did so, and then went for a walk of his own...

CHAPTER 7

Headington, Oxford 1965 Two months later.

Ronald had decided that a short two-week holiday in Scotland, as far away as possible, would be good for him this year. It was ten or eleven years ago he had last been there, that had been the time he stolen for the first time, over a gambling debt that the victim had not paid as he had said he would, that wasn't really stealing, more claiming what was rightfully his. That had all taken place in the Highlands. He rubbed his chin thoughtfully, would anybody remember him? No chance, he thought to himself.

Since he had only the one note with a 'thank you' typed he reasoned that the blackmailer must have been a one off. He had kept his eyes open while out walking, but soon realised that he wouldn't know who the person looked like, so just gave it up as a bad job. He still worked at Merton, on an occasional basis, but was content to live in quiet way. He paid his taxes, and nobody had showed any interest in him or his affairs, well, not until those notes had started to arrive. It would be good to get away he thought to himself as he worked through some essays he was marking. That evening, as he sat reading The Oxford Times, he noticed an article for a hotel in the far north of Scotland, five stars if the article was to be believed. Reaching for his drink, he rose and went to his office to write the cheque and send the booking off before he forgot to do it. He could forget all his worries and relax.

+

Bertie had heard back from the hotel he had seen advertised in The Oxford Times. Set in the far North of Scotland, it was supposed to be five stars. He had written and sent the money a fortnight ago, for two weeks full board, and room with a sea view. Nobody would know him up there, a relaxing break, long overdue, he thought to himself.

CHAPTER 8

East Sutherland Summer 1965

Bill looked across at Jane as the train approached the Mound. He wasn't going to get off here like the last time he thought to himself. The diesel engine was a lot less noisy than the one he had last travelled on.

"It was eleven years ago I last came up here." William said out loud.

"You've told me that already" Jane replied, before going back to reading her magazine. "Do you think it will have changed much?"

"All things change, but it happens at a much slower rate up here." The engine sped along the track towards Golspie.

"Do we get out at Golspie?" She asked.

"No, there is a nearer stop, it's a request stop at the castle."

"Sounds like a bus stop to me."

"We'll ask the conductor at Golspie." The train slowed down as it approached Golspie and came to halt.

"This is Golspie, alight here for Golspie. The conductor said as he walked up and down the train checking to see if anybody was asleep or had left any bags on the train. "Next stop.." Jane interrupted him.

"We want to get off at the Castle. How do we do that?"

"I'll tell the driver, and you press this button here." He pointed to a small yellow button by the door.

"Next stop Dunrobin Castle" The whistle blow and the train started to climb the slow incline up through the fields at the back of the village. After only a few minutes the train started to slow down, Bill got up and pressed the button and as the train pulled into the small station, he leant out of the open window and opened the door. He got out and Jane followed him on to the small platform with a building marked Dunrobin Station. She looked around, nobody else had got off or appeared when the train stopped.

"Where is the ticket office?" she asked Bill.

"There isn't one" he replied. This was built for the Duke of Sutherland. He nodded down through the avenue of trees, That's his home. We have to walk from here, it's around a mile and a half." He bent down and picked up the two suitcases. They set off towards the hotel they had booked for their holiday.

"Romantic holiday you said, nothing mentioned about walking one and a half miles first."

"Look you can see the hotel from here." Bill pointed to the large building on the right, overlooking the North Sea. "It wasn't there, when I last came here, the reviews are very good though, the RAC give it four stars, and the AA five stars."

"Thirty minutes later, they stood in the drive of the hotel. The Broch was situated in the gardens on the left as they looked up the drive. Three stories high, it was made of white stone and slate roof, the door and window frames had been painted with gold paint and the was a neat line of white painted stones each side of the drive leading up to the front door.

"Is it open?" Asked Jane as she gazed with fascination at closed door.

"Should be, they took our deposit cheque and cashed it." Bill replied.

The door opened without a sound as they started to walk up the steps. Inside was a very ornate long hall, with full length draped curtains on the side windows and gold leaf mirrors opposite the windows, giving the appearance of a larger hall. They could just see at the other end, there were two more doors led off the hall, each had a notice over the top of the door, one saying Music Room, and the other The Bar. In between the two doors two very ornate stairways, one on left and one on right spiralled up two more floors with a roof light on the top floor flooding the staircase with light. A lady approached them from a room on the left, just inside the hall.

"You must be Bill and Jane; I will get somebody to show you to your room." She rang a small hand bell, and a man came out and taking their bags indicated they were to follow him to the room.

"Don't we need to sign in?" asked Bill.

"You can do that when you come down later. Now I have put you both in the Sutherland Room. Top floor, overlooking the sea. I hope it's to your liking. It has all the items that you should need. If there is anything you do need, then dial 0 for reception and we'll do our best to help you." With that she went back into the room and Bill and Jane started to climb the winding staircase.

At the top, the landing spread out in a Y shape with two rooms on each side, the doors had names over each one, 'Caithness, Sutherland, Ross-shire,..'

Turning a well-polished brass handle, Bill led Jane into the room. The man coughed slightly as he placed the cases on the purposed built ledge for suitcases.

"I hope this is to your liking?" He said.

"Very much." Replied Bill as he watched Jane run across to a pair of doors on the far side. He reached into his pocket and gave the man a tip. The door closed silently, and they were alone in their room at last.

"This is unbelievable." cried Jane as she sat down on one of four chairs. "Have you seen the bathroom, of course you haven't, it has a roll top bath, and gold taps, two wash basins and everything else you would need. The views are fantastic. Look over here, you can see the train track going north, and there is so much space. While that window overlooks the North Sea. I think I am going to enjoy this holiday." She got up, walked across the room to Bill, and throwing her arms around him, gave him a big kiss.

+

Meantime, In the Ross-shire Suite, Ronald stretched out on his bed. He was on holiday, back in Scotland for the first time since the last time he had been here, the hotel hadn't been built then, when was it? Then he recalled it was way back in the early fifties. He had enjoyed a game of poker in a local hotel. The person he had played had refused to pay at the end of the evening, said it was just a friendly game, and not meant to be for cash. Ronald had been angry, but the man had refused point blank. He had followed him for a couple of days, then, when nobody was watching had taken his chance and hit the man before retrieving the man's wallet and driven off. That was the first time he had stolen, and he found that he enjoyed the thrill of it. Just now and again, not regularly. He had stopped when he got a good job in Oxford, but sometimes had felt he needed the thrill and risk of it. Funny to think that it was here that it had started, he had noticed the stone broch on entering the grounds of the hotel. The location was perfect, nothing to spoil the view, in any of the four directions. He had already gone for a long walk into Golspie and back. Now he was relaxed, nobody would know him here. The worries of Oxford and blackmail notes were left behind. Maybe, he would go and have a drink in the Bar shortly.

In the Caithness Suite, Bertie had just arrived and stood in amazement as he took in the luxury of the rooms, and the views. Why the whole suite was larger than his house in Oxford. That brought a smile to his face, Mr Burgess probably thought that he had heard the last from Bertie, but oh no, this was to be the first of many nice events for Bertie. He walked over to a small table which had a pair of decanters, with a note, 'have a dram on us'. Taking the offer up, he poured a large whisky and sat looking across the North Sea, maybe his next holiday might be further afield, as long as Mr Burgess kept paying. He raised a glass to Mr Burgess and drank it, before pouring a second one.

+

An hour later, Bertie was in the bar, looking at the piano, the bar Manager, came over to him.

"A drink Sir?"

"No thanks, not just yet. Does anybody play?" Nodding at the piano.

"Each night our resident pianist plays a variety of music for the residents." He wiped down the bar, despite the fact that nothing had been spilt, and left Bertie, as another gentleman walked into the room. "What can I get you Sir?"

"Whisky, can you recommend a good one for me to try?"

"Certainly Sir, we have over 50 different ones. I'd recommend 'The Big Burn' it's made by a local firm, based in Golspie. Can be a bit on the strong side for some people though."

"Give me a single of that then please." The man poured a glass and passed it over the counter.

"That will be ten shillings please." A note changed hands, and then Ronald walked over and took a seat near to Bertie, who remained at the bar.

"You on holiday?" Asked Ronald as he looked towards Bertie.

"Yes. Yourself?"

"Just a fortnight, as far away as I can get from Oxford."

"That's funny, I came up from there too." Bertie took another longer look at the man, he looked like, no it was a coincidence, Mr Burgess. "What do you do?"

"I work in the university, at Merton College, do you work there too?" Bertie coughed, as he now realized that it was Burgess. He'd have to be careful that he was not recognized, though as far as Bertie knew, Burgess had no idea of how Bertie looked now.

"No, not nowadays, I retired a few years ago. Still live there though."

"What did you do before you retired? It must have been well paid to afford a holiday here." He gestured with his glass, at the room in general.

"I came into some money, enough for a small holiday."

"Lucky fellow." Ronald drank from his glass, and rose and went back to the barman, "Another of those please." He placed a fiver on the counter and took the glass back along to Bertie. "Have you tried this Whisky yet?"

"Not that one, but I have tried the one in the room decanter. It didn't say where it was made though."

"This is the real stuff; you should try it." He offered his glass to Bertie.

"No thanks, maybe later tonight, I'll be down here for the music.

"Music, what music is that?" Asked Ronald.

"The pianist, he plays each night." Said the bar manager.

"Right, I may be down later. Which part of Oxford do you live in? "

"Headington." Replied Bertie.

"Right, well my name is Ronald, Ronald Burgess." He put out a hand, to shake Bertie's.

"I'm Bertie." He took Ronald's hand and shook it. "Maybe see you later?"

"Maybe." Replied Ronald.

Bertie decided that he should leave, he walked out of the bar and up the stairs to his room. Once inside, he took a minute to think what had just happened. He had come away on holiday, and by a strange coincidence, so had the man he had been blackmailing. He'd have to be careful from now on, or some holiday this would be. Now he wouldn't be so relaxed…

CHAPTER 9

In Brora, Diane Saunders was sitting in the bar of "The Riverside Inn", overlooking the busy harbour, while waiting for the man to meet her. Like a lot of her schemes, getting money from men was easily the best. She started a conversation, took them somewhere for a 'meeting of two lonely people' and once that was done, she would blackmail them for her silence. As long as she kept moving around the country, and didn't do the same scam twice running, then the police were unlikely to catch her. She always looked for men with wedding rings to make things easy. The man she was meeting had had too much whisky and one thing had led to another, and now he had to pay for his mistakes..

Entering the bar, the man looked around and seeing Diane, hurried over to her.

"What is so important it can't wait?" My wife will be wondering where I have got to."

"Ah yes, your wife, would she understand our recent meeting?"

"She would not!"

"Thought as much, so in order that she doesn't I would like for you to give me a regular amount of £5 each month. You can post it to this address." She handed him a brown envelope, already addressed to her PO Box. "You can use cash, and if you keep up the payments, then your wife need never know, however, if the payments were to cease.." She left the sentence unspoken, but the purpose was plain.

"Five pounds! Where do I get five pounds? That's a huge amount. Can't we talk about it first."

"Sure, what do want to say?"

"Three pounds?"

"Five pounds. Talking over, you can start next month." She stood up, indicating the conversation was closed. She finished her drink, and left the bar, leaving him wondering where to get a regular five pounds each month.. He turned to the bar man.

"Any work going in Brora that you know of?" The bar man, looked and slowly wiped down the bar, before speaking.

"I'm looking for somebody to work 2 days each week, can you pull a pint?"

"I'll learn to."

"Then, if you want the job, come over on Monday evening, and I'll show you the ropes, four pounds ten shillings a month. Tips aren't included, so you can earn more if you are good at your job."

"I'll take it." Now he just had to think of a good reason to go out each night two times a week..

+

Diane drove down the road towards Golspie. She approached The Grand East Sutherland Hotel. On impulse she swung left into the drive and parked the car on the right in the small carpark. Walking quickly into the hotel, she made straight for the bar, another hotel, another victim to be played..

+

Ronald stood, slightly unsteadily, and made his way up to his room. How about that, to meet somebody from Oxford, all the way up here.

+

Bertie was thinking, his money wouldn't last as long as he thought, with the prices of things at the hotel. Perhaps he could risk a posted note to Burgess,. no that would be risky, but, there was a 'but', he knew he had paid before, and probably would again. He would have to think carefully, a different approach he thought to himself. An hour later, he had borrowed pen and paper and was printing a note addressed to Mr Burgess.

..You might be on holiday, but I know you wouldn't want anything to spoil it, the first amount was kind, but that was just the first instalment. Leave fifty pounds in a bag, in the centre of the stones..

He took the note, put it in an envelope and having addressed it, took it down to reception, where a postal box was situated. He put it in the box and went back to his room.

+

Flora, hearing the letter box rattle, came out of the reception office. She went to the box, as was her custom, to put the hotel's mail with the post. Seeing the letter addressed to Mr Burgess, she decided to take it to his room. Delivering it would speed up the message rather than taking a day or so to get back to the hotel in the post.

+

Ronald was sat at the desk in his room, Easter Ross, thinking how pleasant the view was, and then he noticed an envelope had been pushed under his door. Curious, he rose and went and retrieved it. Odd, he thought to himself, as he noted that it was stamped, but not cancelled. It was addressed to him, but handwritten. He opened the envelope and took out the short note. Reading it quickly, he screwed it up and tossed it in the bin. How did anybody know he was here? Taking a glass of whisky, he drank it down in one gulp, then gave it a bit more thought, it had to be somebody in the hotel, who thought any post would be at least a day later, by some quirk or other, the letter had been intercepted, and had been delivered early. He gave it some thought, then went down to reception. Ringing the bell, the receptionist appeared.

"Good evening, I wonder if you know who posted this under my door?" He held the envelope up in front of her."

"That would be myself, Mr Burgess. Is there a problem?"

"No problem, I just wondered who would have known me in this hotel, that was all."

"I don't know who posted it, but it can't be that difficult to find out."

"Can you do that?"

"Yes, just give me the envelope." He passed it to her.

"Wait here please." She took the envelope and went back to the office, and then looking at the hotel guest book, compared the writing. She walked back out to Ronald, and smiling, told him that would be Mr Parker. If he wanted to get in touch, he could leave her a note and she would see that Mr Parker would get it.

"No that's fine, I think I may know Mr Parker." He smiled and left the desk. Right, now he knew who the person was, he could stop this before it got a bigger threat. He would have to do this quietly, and without leaving any trace of who, that would not be easy.

CHAPTER 10

Ronald had pondered what to do with Bertie for some while that afternoon. He needed a way of killing him. Though a means without leaving any trace of showing how. Some form of heart attack, or something that would induce it. He suddenly stopped, he recalled reading that there was a couple of plants that might be growing in Scotland, which could be toxic for humans. Now where could he look for that information, he wondered. He went down to reception and asked for directions to the nearest library.

A short while later, he had found what he wanted. A toxic plant, that grew in the Highlands, and even a brush on the skin, would induce heart failure in three hours.

Sheepsbane. A yellow and blue plant with velvet like leaves, found mostly in the North Highlands, its soft leaves are deceptive, as the slightest brush of a leaf against human skin, would start the process of heart failure, something that would take about two to three hours. A rash would appear where the skin and leaf had made contact with the skin, but this will not leave any marks after about two hours.

Perfect, he thought to himself, he put the book back on the shelf, now all he had to do, was to find some of this plant. He had studied the picture of it with care, and now left the library to go outside and see if he could find any.

The gardens of The Grand East Sutherland Hotel, were to say the least, very extensive. They ran south alongside the road, with a mix of fruit, vegetables, and walled gardens. Though it was not here that Ronald concentrated his search, but rather on the boundary, between the hotels grounds and the more rugged north open lands. After about an hour of serious searching, he found what he was looking for. He carefully took a paper bag out of his pocket before pulling it inside out. He placed his hand inside it, and bending down, took a couple of leaves of the deadly plant. Then he turned the bag back on itself, leaving the leaves safely inside. Now all Burgess had to do was to find a way of safely brushing the leaf against the skin of Mr Parker and his problems would be over. Placing the bag carefully into his coat pocket, he started to walk back to the hotel, conscious not to put his hand anywhere near that pocket.

+

Ronald had spent some considerable time manoeuvring the bag of sheepsbane, into a form that he could, still holding the bag, brush a small protruding leaf against anything, like skin for instance. Satisfied, he decided to go down to the music room. He had been promised an evening of entertainment, even if some of that was to be provided by himself.

+

Bertie, before retiring to the music room, made his way to the bar, where perhaps he would try a glass of whisky that Mr Burgess suggested. Approaching the bar, he asked if he could have the same whisky that Mr Burgess had been drinking earlier?

"That will be the 'Big Burn' then." He turned and measured a glass from one of the many bottles behind the bar.

"That's quite a collection you have there. How many different varieties are there?"

"About twenty, a lot of the singles are more recent. The small manufacturer has had its day, the big boys are buying up the small ones, it's cheaper to buy the whole company than just the barrels of whisky." He finished polishing a glass and moved to the next customer. "Mr Burgess, will you be trying a different one, a Glenfiddich perhaps?"

"No, I'll try" he hesitated, "Why don't you surprise me?" Turning to Bertie, he slapped him lightly on the back, near his neck, saying, "How about you, do you want a drink?" Ronald replaced his hand carefully back into the pocket and smiled at the bar manager.

"Not for me thank you, just started this one," He raised his glass, 'Cheers', then Bertie made his way through to the music room and took a chair by the window. Ronald looked in, then took a chair nearer the door, he wanted to be able to leave without making a fuss, or anybody really noticing he thought to himself.

+

Diane, seated across the room, had seen exactly what he had done, even down to the bit of plant sticking out of the bag in his hand. Well, well she thought to herself, maybe this might be worth staying around for, she rose, walked past Ronald without a glance and went to arrange a stay for a week or so.

+

That evening after Dinner, Jane and Bill walked through to the Music room. The walls were decorated with green and gold wallpaper. In the corner was a Grand Piano, the pianist was softly playing 'Moonlight Sonata'. The room had quite a number of the hotels guests sat in very comfy chairs and settees scattered between the chairs were small tables. Bill looked around the room.

"Where do you get a drink?"

"Through the door over there" Jane replied. "The one with the sign saying BAR over it." She smiled at him, as he got up and walked over to the door, then walked back to her.

"What do you want to drink?"

"Gin and Orange please." He walked back to the Bar and ordered the drinks. A short while later a waiter brought them over to their table. Bill nodded towards a gentleman sat near one of the windows, on the windowsill sat a one of the new Lava Lamps, but not working.

"I wonder why that is not working?"

"What isn't working?"

"The Lava Lamp, they are all the rage, and yet it isn't lit."

"Perhaps it is not plugged in, or something, does it really matter?"

"Suppose not, just wondered. Nice drink?"

"Yes, very nice."They sat back and enjoyed the music being played in the background. As the evening wore on, the room got a bit busier, and people kept pushing past them and the gentleman sat in the chair by the window as they went to and from the Bar. By the end of the evening, most of the guests had left the room and the pianist had packed up his music and left the room as well. Bill and Jane were getting up to go to their room, when Bill nudged Jane.

"He hasn't moved all night, and his head has fallen forward."

"He is asleep." Jane answered with a smile. "The music probably sent him off. Come on, it's our turn to go to bed."William bent down to see if she was right, and if the man was asleep, but from the colour of the man's face, it didn't look as though he was asleep.

"I think he is ill." Hissed Bill at Jane, "I am going to speak to somebody about him."

"Ok, but I am going on up to bed. I'll see you shortly." Jane made her way passed them both and up the stairway to their room.

Bill walked quickly through to the reception area, and almost at once the lady who had greeted them on their arrival, appeared.

"Is there anything I can do to help you?" She asked.

"There is a guest in the music room who appears to be ill, can you call somebody to see to him please?" asked Bill.

"Of course, I'll phone for a Doctor to come out and see him." She turned and went back to the office to phone.

CHAPTER 11

An hour later, the Doctor had come, declared the man had died, and the police had been summoned. The receptionist opened the door to the policeman who was coming up the stairs.

"Do come in, Constable?"

"DI Gray, and you are?" He said as he took out his notebook.

"Miss Sutherland, Receptionist and hotel under manager. I phoned for the Doctor after a guest had reported seeing another guest not well."

"Thank you Miss Sutherland, I'll probably be needing to arrange for somebody to take your statement in due course. Who was it that discovered the body?"

"Mr Dawson, he is a guest, staying here with Miss Rose, they are in the Sutherland Suite. It's on the second floor, I can show you if you want?"

"Thank you, but first I want to see where the person was found, the music room I think?"

"That's right, go along the hall, and it's the room on the right at the end, next to the Bar." Flora watched as he walked briskly along the hall towards the Music Room where poor Mr Parker had been found dead. Still, it's very unusual for a guest to die like that, she thought to herself as she turned to go back to the office.

+

DI Gray walked into the music room, looking around as he did so. It struck him that most people would have been able to see where Mr Parker had died. He walked over to the chair, now covered with a dustsheet, and carefully removed it. No stains on the chair or the floor, he thought to himself as he tilted the chair back on its two rear legs. Replacing the chair as he had found it, he walked over to the piano, and ran his fingers along the keyboard. He wished he could play, but that was not possible with the hundred and one other things he had to do. Leaving the room, he made his way back to the reception and thought to himself that it was just an accident. He would get some statements taken from the guests in the room, better to be safe than sorry he thought. At reception, he asked if he could phone to get a Sergeant to come and take some statements from the guests.

+

The following morning, DI Gray sat in his office, looking through the statements that the Sergeant had taken from the guests last night and into the early hours of this morning, They had been typed up and carbon copies sent to the Division headquarters, just in case, he thought to himself. The post-mortem had been carried out, and it had been decided that heart failure was the probable cause of death, at least that was what had been declared. Most of the guests hadn't recalled paying any attention to Mr Parker, and a lot had left the room before Mr Dawson had discovered the body. At present it appeared that only the pianist and Mr Dawson were the only two people who had been in the room when Mr Parker had died, at least that what he thought. He opened the drawer to the desk and nearly took out the packet of cigars that lay inside, then he shut the desk drawer, and got up, and grabbing a coat, walked quickly out to the front desk.

"I am going back to the Grand East Sutherland Hotel, if anybody wants me, they can phone or leave a message there."

"Is there anything wrong?"

"No, it's just to tell them it was heart failure, and that we are not investigating further."

"Ok sir." The desk Sergeant went back to his paperwork, choosing the place to put the X in that week's Spot the ball competition.

+

Six days later..

Ronald was pleased with himself, he had got away with murder, literally, he had a week of living on his nerves, as the police had searched for any reason or clue but the death had been put down to heart attack. Having got rid of the rest of the plant safely, was now enjoying the rest of his holiday. Strolling in the garden on his way toward the Broch. A lady, dressed for the outdoors, approached him.

"Mr Burgess isn't it?"

"Yes, do I know you?"

"No, but you will soon." She turned and started to walk away. He gazed after her. I wonder what she meant by that he thought. Then continued to walk in the opposite direction.

+

Diane was pleased with how that initial meeting had gone. She had Burgess hooked but he didn't realise it yet. She would have to be very careful with this one, opportunities like this didn't present themselves every day. Maybe a short note, under his door may be the answer. Making her way to her room, she started to think what to write..

..An hour later, she reread the note, and pleased with herself, tucked it into the hotel blue envelope, that matched the paper and leaving her room, went to reception to ask if it could be taken to Mr Burgess please?

"Certainly. I'll get somebody to run it to him now shall I?"

"Appreciated". Diane took a ten shilling note and passed it to Flora, and this is for you." She nodded her head in a sideways manner, as though saying not a word to anybody.

"Appreciate it. Thank you very much."The ten shilling note was exchanged, and quickly slipped into the handbag of Flora. Diane left and made her way to the bar; she needed a drink.

+

Ronald was stood on top of the Broch. He watched as he saw a young person coming out of the hotel carrying a letter or something and looking around as though looking for somebody. He started to climb down and walk back to the hotel, the view was not so good today, but still worth the walk. Once in the hotel, he was approached by the young person.

"Mr Burgess?"

"Yes?"

"A letter for you sir." He handed the note to Burgess, who noted it was not stuck down or addressed in any way.

"How did you know it was for me?"

"I was told to give it to you by Miss Sutherland, Sir."

"Have you read it?"

"Of course not." But his red face told a different tale.

"Well then, here is a tip for your trouble." He passed a tip over to him and watched as he left the Broch and smiled to himself, before taking the message out of the envelope.

Mr Burgess, I will say nothing of the dreadful deed that you have committed here in the hotel, providing you pay a small regular amount to me each month. I am sure that you don't want the police involved in anyway do you? This will stay just between the two of us. I think that about £15 each month would cover it for now.. Leave a note under the door of my room with your answer, by six tonight.

He gasped out loud, why, oh, why did this happen to him? Where would he now get another fifteen pounds each month? He would have to reason with the person. Though the thoughts of reasoning with another blackmailer made him shudder. It had quite spoilt his holiday. As he started back to the hotel, a thought passed his mind, the young man who had brought the note, he would know as well, Damn! Now two people know, this was becoming a bigger problem. He had thought he that getting rid of Bertie would solve the problem. Instead it seemed to be like horrid version of the Hydra in Greek mythology. Get rid of one person and two appear instead. Once in the hotel, he went and quickly replied, before sticking it under the door of the room concerned. Diane was waiting in her room saw the note and quickly picked it up and opening it, read it quickly, before a smile crossed her face, he was clever, that was a fact. She re-read it again..

I know what you plan to do but I think that we are not the only two people to know what might have occurred, the bearer of the note probably has read it, and so your attempt at a large regular amount is not really worth what you think. Let's meet and discuss what you think you saw; I'll be in the library from six tonight.

+

Bill and Jane were outside walking in the garden. They approached the Broch and Bill stopped for a few minutes.

"Bill, what is it?" asked Jane.

"Just time standing still, just being silly probably."

"Tell me, what is wrong?"

"Nothing's wrong, well not now anyhow, it was seeing this Broch, it brought it all back to me."

"Now you are worrying me, come over here, sit down and tell me the whole tale."

"If you insist."

"I do."

"Right then, where to start, it was like this, I was on holiday up here with my parents. It was when I was about 10 years old. We had hired a car and had driven around to Golspie and then onwards to this spot to have a picnic."

"A picnic, is that what this is all about?"

"Not exactly, we had had that, and I was exploring, then I saw a man knock another man to the ground and steal his wallet."

"Did you tell the police?"

"I told my parents, but by the time they came to have a look, both men had disappeared. My father thought I had made it all up, but I hadn't, I think that I would know either of the two men If I ever saw them again. Seeing it again has brought it all back to me. You must think me very silly."

"Not at all, seeing something like that is bound to make a lasting impression." She leant towards him and gave him a peck on the cheek. They both stood and carried on walking in the extensive gardens.

"It's been a very pleasant week, apart from that first evening, when you found the dead man."

"You mean Mr Parker." Said Bill with a frown. "The police have said it was not foul play, he just died."

"We all do that eventually, but I know you think I should forget all about it."

"Yes, I do think that, and we have another week to look forward to. Where do you think we should go next week, now that we have explored Wick and Thurso?"

"Well, I 'll have to think about that, perhaps over dinner tonight we can discuss it further?" She smiled at him as she reached for his hand.

"And after Dinner?" Bill asked playfully.

"Listen to the Pianist in the music room. He was a good player last week."

"I was thinking.."

"Oh, that makes a change." Jane butted in with a laugh. "Ok, what were you thinking?"

"Whatever happened to the two men I saw all those years ago."

"Well, whatever did happen, I am sure that they are not around here now."

CHAPTER 12

Later that night Ronald sat in the semi lit library, wondering if the blackmailer would have the nerve to show up. By the time the black marble clock on the mantlepiece struck seven, he had resigned himself to knowing that they wouldn't show now, when there was a tap on the door.

"Come in." The door opened slowly and then the young man who had handed him the note stuck his head around the door.

"I have a note for you Mr Burgess." A hand appeared holding the note. Ronald rose, and taking the note from the young man, nodded as if to say, you can go now. The hand and head withdrew from sight and the door closed again. Ronald noted this time the envelope was sealed, tearing the envelope open, he took out the note, and read it.

"Really Mr Burgess, did you think I would fall for that suggestion? Ok, so maybe you are right, £15 is too much, this is my final demand £12 a month or £100 as a lump sum once a year. There, I can't be fairer than that, a saving for you of £44 a year. Now simply leave the money in an envelope addressed to Ruth Mitchell, Poste Restante, Dornoch Post Office, The Square, Dornoch, Sutherland, Scotland. Don't try and follow me, or go to the police or I will get very angry indeed, and you would not want that now, would you? Don't worry about the other person, they will keep quiet.."

+

Bill and Jane made their way to the music room. They had eaten a nice dinner and now were planning a nice relaxing evening. The Music room had a few people seated around the small tables, but nobody was at the piano.

"Wonder where the pianist is tonight?" said Bill.

"Could be off sick?"

"Suppose so. Still you would think that they would have a notice or something saying so." At that a young man, with glasses walked into the room and looked around before making his way to the piano. He turned to the cupboard to the left of the piano, and took out some music, looking through it, he selected one piece and turned to start to play moonlight sonata 3rd movement. Jane groaned, at which the pianist stopped playing and looked over towards Jane.

"Something the matter?" He asked.

"Only that was what the pianist played last week. Do you know anything else?"

"What do you have in mind?"

"Anything more modern" said Jane.

"Well, I do know some modern music but does anybody else want that played." He looked around the room, and nobody said no, so he started playing it. At the end everybody applauded, and he asked if there were any other requests. A few hands shot up to make suggestions. As the evening wore on, and he played the request one after another he appeared to take all of them in his stride.

+

Ronald, his hands shaking, reread the note for the third time. As he paced the room a loud scream filled the hotel. Tossing the note onto the table, he opened the door and looked up and down the corridor, nobody was in sight. Then voices seemed to rise from the stairwell. He walked over, and peering down, saw a body spread-eagled on the floor. Running quickly down the stairs he forgot all about the note.

+

Bill was in the Bar, when suddenly a loud scream ran through the building. Everybody stood and started to move towards the door, but Bill, being nearest, dashed out to the hall to find a young man lying face up at the bottom of the stairs in a grotesque twisted position. Other guests were coming through from the music room, Burgess stopped as he reached the bottom of the stairs. He put his hand out to stop anybody else from coming through.

"Don't think anybody could help him, he looks dead to me." One of the onlookers muttered quietly. Jane had followed the rest of the guests out of the Music room, and now made her way over to Bill.

"What happened?" Asked Flora, who had appeared from reception.

"Don't know, it looks as though it he just fell, the police will sort it out."

"The Police?" she raised a hand to her mouth. "I hadn't thought about them. This will be the second time they will have been called by the hotel."

"Well they will have to be called, unexpected death and all that.."

"Ok, the rest of you please stand back, I'll go and call the Police, Mr Dawson, can you make sure nobody touches Mr Ross please until they get here." She walked off towards her office. The other guests on hearing her had started to drift back to the various rooms that they had been in before they had heard the loud scream.

+

A short time later DS Cooper made his way over towards Bill. He nodded towards the stairs.

"He fell?"

"Don't know, I was in the bar and heard a scream, ran out in the direction of it, and found him like this."

"Have you touched him or anybody else for that matter?"

"No, the receptionist asked me to stay and make sure that nobody came near it. So that is what I have done."

"Getting quite a habit here isn't it, you, finding the dead bodies"

"Now wait a minute, I only came out as I heard the scream. You are not suggesting that I had anything to do with it are you?" Bill looked at the policeman.

"Until I have a statement from everybody as to their whereabouts, I am not ruling anybody in or out." He said with emphasis. "Now Sir, what exactly did you hear? Take your time." He took a notebook and pencil out and waited for Bill to speak.

"Both myself and Jane had gone to the music room after dinner, I had gone to the bar to get our drinks, heard a scream, and went straight to where the sound seemed to come from, the hall, and found this man as you see him. A lot of guests came out of the rooms they were in at the time. That's about it really."

"Did you see anybody upstairs?"

"I didn't look, I was too busy looking at the body. Why?"

"Just wondered." He put away his notebook and pencil and looked at the stairway spiralling upwards above them. Turning to Bill he said, "Can you make sure nobody follows me upstairs please?" Then Cooper turned and went up the stairs, slowly looking over the handrail as he did so. He reached the second landing and looked downwards. Then he returned to the bottom of the stairs, by which time the ambulance had arrived and so had the Doctor. "Well Doctor, how did he die?"

"I can't tell you that now, too many bruises and cuts, I'll have a better idea once the PM is carried out."

"Best guess then," DS Cooper stopped and looked over to Bill, "Best you go off now. You've been very helpful, but don't assume I have ruled you out or in at the moment. Don't leave the hotel grounds at the moment, unless you have spoken to me first, understand?"

"Yes. So, I can go now then?"

"That's what I said." Cooper turned his attention to the Doctor again and lowered his voice. "Your best guess, am I dealing with another accident or murder?"

"Treat as Murder and hope for accident." The Doctor straightened his back, and picking up his case, took a quick glance at the body, and left the hall. As the Doctor approached the front door, he turned to the policeman, you can move the body now." Then he walked out to his car on the drive.

Cooper stooped down and looked closely at the left hand of the dead man. It was clenched as a fist, and running through it, he could just make out a small piece of red material. He didn't move it, then, taking another look up the winding stairs to the landing on the second floor, he could just make out the full-length red curtains hanging by the window. He turned back to the reception desk.

"Could you please phone Dornoch Police and ask that DI Gray comes to the hotel urgently, and to bring some back up as well."

"Yes, I'll do that, urgent you say?"

"Very, and nobody is to go up the stair on the left hand side, looking from the front door, do you understand?"

"Yes." She picked up the phone and started dialling the number for Dornoch Police.

+

DI Gray had arrived half an hour later along with a couple of other police-men, who were now in the bar and music room. The assembled guests looked up from their drinks as he appeared at the door of the music room.

"I'll need statements from all of you, the officers will speak to you one at a time, so until your name is called, please stay here." He nodded to the pianist, "Play something relaxing in the meantime please!" He turned and left the room. Bending down to pick up some music that had drifted to the floor, the pianist started to play softly…

+

Once Gray had left the room, he turned to Cooper and motioned to follow him upstairs. Taking the right hand side, they quickly reached the top, and DI Gray looked over the rails at the scene below, a chalked outline of the body was on the floor.

"Face upwards you say?"

"Yes, and the Doctor said he could not see anything obvious that caused his death so he must have just fallen."

"Tell me Cooper, how many times do you just fall?" Gray looked at his Ser-geant and grinned. "He must have either been pushed or tripped. So, let's look at the curtains, and anything else that might have tripped him up." Gray moved towards the full-length curtain at the top of the stairs where Sidney had fallen.

"Sir."

"What is it?"

"He had this red thread in his hand." Cooper passed the thread over to Gray, who taking it, looked at the curtain and then the thread.

"It's the same colour, take a closer look, is there a thread missing anywhere from the curtain?" Both stooped down and looked closely, but nothing was missing from the curtain that they could see.

"There are lots of red curtains in the hotel, take a look at all the windows, they have the same material. I bet that the housekeeper keeps the matching thread to repair any that get damaged." Said Cooper excitedly.

"Well, it would take a long time to check all of them, maybe it's a red thread herring?" Cooper groaned at the awful pun and grasped the railing as he looked down again at the scene below. He felt that his hand had grabbed something sticky, he let go of the railing and looked at it, it was pale red. He looked across to DI Gray who was now on his knees looking at something on the floor.

"Sir, could this be blood?" He held his hand up to show him. DI Gray got up and came over to take a closer look.

"Where did you get this on your hand?"

"Must be when I grabbed the railing, here." He pointed at the rail and saw a smudge of light red on the brass rail.

"Has that Doctor gone yet?" Asked DI Gray .

"Yes, why?"

"I wanted him to check this, to see if it matches the blood of the victim. Let's seal off this part of the stairs and get him to come back later and take a sample of this." If it matches, then he was injured before he fell. Why did he die?" DI Gray stood and looked first down and then across the hall to reception and then up at the doors to the rooms on the first floor. "Let's also find out who is in these rooms and also if anybody was in the library at the time."

"Did you see anything on the floor Sir?"

"No, nothing at all." DI Gray stood and stretched, then walked down to the main hall. "Look, I'm heading back, you get the statements together, see if anything leaps out as to why the poor man had to be killed, and get somebody to keep watch on that handrail overnight, I don't want it washed away by some zealous housekeeper. It may be evidence worth keeping." Cooper nodded and turned to the music room as DI Gray left the hotel.

CHAPTER 13

The following morning DI Gray was in his office talking on the phone to the Doctor who had carried out the PM. He tapped his pen on the pad of paper in front of him impatiently waiting for the Doctor to finish speaking.

"So, what you are saying Doctor, is that you cannot say for certain if it was an accident or murder? Are there too many cuts and bruises to the body to clearly define which it was?"

"Exactly so. I'm sorry I cannot be more decisive in my conclusions. I can tell you that the blood on the railings was the victims."

"Do we have a name for the man yet?"

"Yes, it was a member of staff, just a moment," there was the sound of rustling papers, "ah, here it is. Mr Sidney Ross, worked at the hotel." DI Gray gripped the phone tightly.

"Who identified him?"

"We got that from his wallet, there was a hotel pass in it."

"So, no actual person has identified him yet?"

"No, not as such. Why is it important?"

"It might be, look thanks for that, I'll get back to you soon." With that DI Gray hung up, just as his office door got knocked. "Come in."

Sergeant Cooper came into the room. It was obvious to DI Gray that something significant had occurred. "Well, what is it?"

"A piece of material was torn from a curtain on the First floor landing by the window."

"First floor you say?"

"Yes, but there is a problem."

"Which is?"

"She noticed it the day before, and had it taken down and replaced, it, the damaged one, is waiting for her to repair. She thinks it must have been jerked hard for it to have ripped the material as well. I have looked at it closely under a microscope and there is no clean edge, so it must have been pulled, rather than cut."

"I wonder if that gave our murder an idea?"

"Well, if it did, there was no sign of any torn curtain yesterday. By the way, somebody has been and taken a sample of the blood on the rail, they said they will get back to us as soon as they can, but they have a backlog of work to do first."

"They must have worked fast, the Doctor has confirmed the blood as belonging to the victim."

"Oh."

"So, we are no further forward then?" said DI Gray .

"Have you spoken to the Doctor yet?"

"Yes, just got off the phone, he said that there are too many cuts and bruises to say if any particular one was the cause of it." Cooper stood looking a little deflated, he said nothing, he knew of past experience, that if DI Gray was silent, then he was thinking, and didn't like being interrupted.

. DI Gray sat thinking that if it was murder, then there appeared to be nothing to prove it. The pile of witness statements, taken last night, or early this morning, he thought to himself, accounted for everybody that could be contacted in the hotel. A lot of the guests had been in the Music room or the bar, so easily had given alibis to other guests, the receptionist, what was her name, he thought to himself, as he rummaged through the statements to find hers, Flora, that was it. Satisfied that he had found her statement he sat back and reread it to himself, it appeared quite acceptable, except that she had been by herself. He felt that he was overlooking something or somebody. He got up and made his way over to the door, maybe a trip to the hotel might jerk his memory.

"Come on, let's go back to the hotel." He left the office with Cooper shutting the door behind him. Both of them went down to his car and drove off towards the hotel.

+

At the same time DI Gray and DS Cooper were driving to the hotel. Jane and Bill were finishing breakfast there. Bill finished his tea, and looked over to Jane, who was reading the paper. The paper headline was about some strike or other that was going to affect everybody, if the paper was to be believed. Jane was engrossed in something in the inside pages. He coughed quietly. Jane looked over the top of the paper.

"Yes?"

"Have you finished breakfast?" She glanced down at her plate, with its remaining toast, now cold, and nodded.

"Yes, I was reading about Inverness, there is a new exhibition opening to-morrow, and I wondered if we should go to it."

"That is quite a walk, first from here to Golspie. Then by train to Inverness which loops around Loch Fleet. On through Lairg and Ardgay, before heading to Inverness. I'll check the timetables but think we would take a good three hours each way, six in total, and not very long to see your exhibition."

"Oh, I hadn't thought about the amount of time to travel. Bother." He waited, knowing that she hadn't finished. "Bill, while the hotel is very grand and nice, there have been two deaths and I wonder if we checked out and went to Inverness we could stay in some hotel there for the rest of the holiday."

"I can find out if you really want to do that. Look, why don't we stay for the moment. I'll go and find out what the situation is and if we can leave the hotel, we could go tomorrow morning. We'll get up early and catch an early train and so on. What do you think?"

"Ok, you go and find out, and I'll go and sit in the grounds. It's lovely and sunny after all."

"Well wrap up warm, it may be cold outside."

"It's summer, it'll be hot."

"Don't say I didn't warn you then." Bill rose and headed towards the re-ception area by the front door.

DI Gray pulled up outside the front door, and quickly walked up the steps and into the hotel. He noticed Bill was walking towards reception. They met, and smiled at each other, then both started to go to the bell, DI Gray stepped back.

"After you." Gray said.

"Thanks, but you probably need it first, I can wait."

"I may be some time, you go first." Bill stepped up the desk as the recep-tionist came out to greet them both.

"Now which of you two gentlemen do I speak to first?"

"Him," said DI Gray , nodding in the direction of Bill.

"Ok, what can I do for you Mr Dawson?"

"I know I booked for two weeks, but Jane is wondering about going to In-verness, and with the two deaths." his voice trailed off.

"I quite understand, you want to cut short the break, one of the other guests has already asked me the same question. You can cut short the booking, but you would only get half your remaining money back. We would not be able to use the room you see. Are you sure you want to surrender the room?"

"I'll go and talk to Jane, see what she thinks, oh by the way, do you have a train timetable by any chance?" She looked under the desk, and produced, a train timetable.

"It's the last one. Here you are." Handing it over, Bill took it and left. Turning to the receptionist, DI Gray noticed it wasn't Flora.

"Miss Sutherland not around?"

"No, she was shaken by the death yesterday, the manager gave her the day off. What was it you wanted Officer?"

"When did you give out the previous timetable before that one?"

"Well, to tell you the truth, I thought we had more than that, I am surprised that we only had that one left."

"But when did you give the others away, and to who?"

"I can't remember. Why is it important?"

"It might be, have a think about it and let me know. You know the number to phone?"

"Yes, Miss Sutherland left it here." She smiled at DI Gray and produced a bit of paper. "What was it what you wanted today anyhow?"

"I want to have another look at the stairs if that is possible please?"

"Of course, we stopped people coming down the side that was used by poor Mr Ross, you know the way." She stepped back into her office. DI Gray stepped along the hall and took the stairs on the right hand side. He made his way to the top of the stairwell on the second floor. Then walked down the other staircase, carefully looking at each step. When he came to the first floor, he looked at the curtain that Cooper had mentioned, rightly enough, no tear or marks. What then had made the young man fall? DI Gray walked down the stairwell, the area where the body had landed had been cordoned off and took another look at the step and banister rail. Nothing appeared out of the ordinary. But I don't know what ordinary was, he thought to himself. He decided that he would tell both his superiors and Miss Sutherland that it was just another accident.

CHAPTER 14

Upstairs Bill was talking to Jane about what the hotel had said regarding the giving up of the suite.

"I don't mind giving it up, as long as you are happy, that is more important to me."

"Well I think that I could live with one death, but two in the space of a week. I'd rather go to Inverness."

"Ok, we'll go tomorrow, I have the timetable for the trains, there is a very early one, goes from Dunrobin around 8.00 in the morning, so we could be in Inverness by 10.00. That takes care of tomorrow, now what about today?"

"Fancy a walk?" Jane asked.

"To the station you mean?"

"No, I was looking at some leaflets, and there is a walk up to the monument in Golspie, it takes around 3 hours up and back. It looks easy to do. The views would be great from the top."

"It would give us some air I suppose." He looked down at Jane and smiled. "Come on then, the sooner we start the better."

"I'll just get a coat." Jane went over and selected a green top jacket. Bill grabbed his leather jacket off the back of the chair. Half an hour later they arrived on the outskirts of Golspie. They saw the Sutherland Inn and carried on towards the main centre of the village. The range of shops running both sides of the street, with lots of people out and about, gave a buzz to the place. Bill looked at the leaflet that Jane had given him. The walk was clearly marked out. Once in the centre of the village, they turned to the right and walked up the street to a fountain at the top of the street. Under the railway bridge, and up through the farm, signs were posted here and there marked with 'To the top' or 'This way to the Ben' This made it easier to follow the path. To start with it climbed easily through wooded areas then started to get steeper, they crossed a wide track, and made their way, more slowly now, up the steeper climb, onwards into view of the monument, but stopping now and then to take a breath or look back at the village and the hotel in the distance. They could make out the snaking railway line running alongside the main road, heading its way northwards.

"Come on Bill, just a bit further to go, you can see the top from here." Bill glanced up from where he had stopped to take breath, sure enough the monument loomed over them, the deep blue sky highlighting the outline of the statue. Taking a deep breath, he set off for the last few yards, following Jane on up and finally, stopping at the red sandstone base, where Jane stood looking back at him.

"You made it then?"

He puffed, and bending over, got his breath back.

"I thought I was fit, but that is a killer of a walk."

"We are not at the top yet."

"What!" Bill exclaimed.

"Don't worry, look it rises a bit more then slopes downwards through the gorse on the other side of the hill." She pointed up ahead and sure enough, it did rise a bit more. He gazed at the view and then looking at the base of the statue. Wondering to himself, how on earth did they get the materials up here and then build it as well? Jane shouted back, and he looked ahead and saw she had reached the summit of the hill. It seemed so much more than a hill! Jane shouted again, and he moved quickly over the much easier ground. Reaching Jane, he put his arm around her:

"The view is fantastic, but that wind is cruel."

"I agree. I should have brought the camera, but it is back at the hotel. Never mind we will have to remember it. Shall we start back down?" She asked him.

"Might as well. It will take us a lot less time going back down, how long did it take us to get here?"

"Well, it took us 40 minutes to get to the village from the hotel, and.." She stopped to look at her watch.. "About two hours from the village. It shouldn't take that long to get back to the village though. Come on." She started to stride back towards the monument. Bill started after her, heading back down the way they had come. He caught her up and managed to squeeze past her.

"Keep up!" He shouted above the wind.

Jane followed, now more slowly, than when she had climbed up here..

..Forty minutes later found them both walking through the farm and on down to the village.

"What a view that was, all ways North, South, West." She said.

"Not East though, that is just the sea. I just wonder why the statue faces out to the sea."

"Yes, now you mention it, it does seem odd. Though the village can see him from here, look." She pointed up at the statue. "There must be a reason for it, we'll ask in the hotel or in Inverness."

"We could go to the station and get our tickets for tomorrow. While we are in the village. It would save time tomorrow, especially as there is no booking office at the castle halt."

"Onwards then, ever onwards." Jane sighed as they turned right onto the main road and walked on towards Golspie railway station.

Ten minutes later, they had bought their tickets, and were stood outside the station, looking at each other.

"Back to the hotel then." Asked Bill.

"We could see if there is anywhere to eat in the village for lunch?"

"Good idea, do you remember anywhere when we walked in?"

"Not really, but we can look as we walk back, can't we?" They set off and walked on the sunny side of the main road, passing a baker's and a small range of independent shops that ran on both sides of the street. They passed a couple of small hotels, but nothing offering lunch. Shortly, they had reached the end of the street, and were turning by the church back towards the hotel. "Look, we could see if we can eat at that hotel, next to the petrol station." Jane pointed up the road towards the hotel. "Come on, bet there will be food there." They started walking towards it.

+

Ronald sat in the garden. His head in his hands, what was he to do? The money was a problem, but how to deal with a blackmailer who was obviously as ruthless as they had said. He was in no doubt that the death of the young man was no accident. If they could kill easily, then what choice did he have but to pay up? He couldn't go to the police. To do that would open a huge can of worms and he would end up in prison, and no job or pension. He couldn't appeal to the blackmailers better nature. The murder of the young man had proved they didn't have one. He shuddered as he recalled the shout and the sound of the thud of the body hitting the floor of the hotel.

+

Diane was walking towards him, a smile crossing her face as she approached him. She sat down beside him.

"Are you ok?" Diane asked.

"Yes, quite alright." Replied Ronald without looking at her.

"You don't look it. Do you want me to get somebody?"

"No, sorry I am a bit upset, some bad news that's all."

"Well if you are sure." Diane rose and carried on walking in the gardens, before turning back to the hotel.

In the hotel, Sarah Peters, one of the many cleaners the hotel employed, was having a bad morning. She had been told to clear some of the older items in the library out and put them in the attic for storage. This was after she had cleaned and tidied the suites that she had responsibility for. It was too bad, she had had quite a soft spot for Sidney, and it had really shaken her that he had died so young. Dabbing her eyes, she finished cleaning the last of the suites. Right, she thought to herself, I wonder what the Library has in store for me. With a determined walk, she put her cleaning materials away in the cupboard just off the landing and walked towards the library.

Inside a number of items from around the hotel, had been gathered together in front of the desk and a table had been pushed up against it, to make room for the items. Sarah pushed open the door, and looked in, she groaned, closed the door, and went down to reception.

Ringing the bell, Flora came out from her office.

"Yes Sarah?"

"I think you said to clear the library of the items that need to go into the attic?"

"Yes, that's right. Is there a problem?"

"Well, some of them are rather on the large size, and I would need somebody else to help up the stairs with them, I would have normally asked,.." She broke off and sniffed into hanky.

"Yes, alright, I'll send somebody along to help, now you start moving the items you can manage, nearer to the attic stairs."

"Thank you." Sarah turned and went back to the library and started to move the smaller items. Half an hour later, only four larger items remained. She took a break, and sat at the desk, her eye, catching sight of a blue screwed-up paper lying on the table in front of her, curious now, she got up and went to see what it was. Just as she bent down and picked up the paper, the door opened, but Sarah didn't notice it, she was busy reading the paper..

"Really Mr Burgess, did you think I would fall for that suggestion? Ok, so maybe you are right, £15 is too much, this is my final demand £12 a month or £100 as a lump sum once a year. There, I can't be fairer than that, a saving of £44 a year. Now simply leave the money in an envelope addressed to Ruth Mitchell, Poste Restante, Dornoch Post Office, The Square, Dornoch, Sutherland, Scotland. Don't try to follow

me, or go to the police or I will get very angry indeed, and you would not want that now, would you? Don't worry about the other person, they will keep quiet."

Diane came into the room, noticing that a young lady was reading something on a blue piece of paper, she approached her slowly and quietly. Sarah gave a small cry as she realised she had company, putting the note back down on the desk, she turned to Diane.

"Can I help you? Or are you here to help me?" She smiled.

"Maybe I can help you? What were you reading when I came in?"

"Oh that, nothing important really, I am expecting some help to move these few items up to the attic. I was just being nosey." She smiled at Diane.

"Nosey, well I expect we all can be that at times. What about?"

"Nothing really important, I'll come back and let you get on." Sarah scooped the paper into her hand and pushed it into the front pocket of her uniform. All the while Diane looked on, beginning to think that it may be the note she had written, how many bits of blue paper would be around in the hotel. She smiled at Sarah.

"I could help you get those things to the attic if you want?"

"Oh no, I couldn't ask a guest to help, that is more than my job is worth. I'll go and find somebody." She turned to leave the room.

"Nonsense, it would only take a few minutes, then it is done. Come on, which is the first one, this one?" She bent over and started to lift a large heavy statue of a woman carrying a baby on her back, it was obviously too heavy for one person, so automatically, Sarah went and helped, and they both walked up the stairs to the Attic door, which was now open, revealing a further flight of stairs going upwards. Diane lead the way, and soon was in a dry boarded attic space with a chair, floor lamp and some cushions arranged on the floor. "Quite a home from home isn't it?"

"It's where staff can relax, we don't have a staff room as such, it doesn't get used much, it's too far up for us." They went down and brought up the other three pieces, then while they stood getting their breath back, Sarah brought back out the note and re-read it. "I think I will show this to Flora, she will know what to do. It looks like some sort of threat against somebody else. I am sure the police will want to know too."

"Here, let me have a look, I may be able to help in some way."

"Alright, here you take a look, it sounds so, well, threatening, don't you think?" Diane took the proffered paper and started to read. It was her note, this needed to be sorted, and quickly too. She looked up as the door opened behind her.

"Sarah, did you get the help I sent up?" Said Flora as she entered the room.

"No, Miss Sutherland."

"Well, I can see you have finished anyhow, so can you come along and help to change the IONA Suite, the guest doesn't like the view, so am having to move them to SKYE suite instead." Flora turned and left the Library.

"Look, thanks for letting me read the note. You give it some thought, and I'll do the same and meet up again, say in the attic about two hours from now?" Said Diane.

Sarah looked at Diane and then at her watch. "Ok, two hours' time. Now I really must get on." With that she left Diana alone in the Library thinking what was she to do about Sarah?

Diane sat down at the desk, she wondered if she should cut and run now. Sarah wasn't stupid though, if she did that she would soon get caught. No, a more permanent solution needed to be found. She sat and thought for quite a while. Rising from the chair, she went out and up the next flight of stairs to the top floor. The attic door was now closed. After looking both right and left, she swiftly made her way towards it and went inside. The lights were still on, so she closed the door and went up the stairs. An idea had occurred to her from something she thought she had seen in the attic last time. She made her way over to the chair, and sure enough there sat a lava lamp but it wasn't plugged in., She spied a socket and took the lamp over and plugged it in. It started to glow red, but nothing happened inside. Bother, thought Diane to herself, it doesn't seem to work. She sat down and thought some more as to what to do with Sarah.

Half an hour later, she stood up and noticed the lamp was now moving the wax inside it up, and down as it should. Oh, that was good. Now all she needed was a bucket, and a cloth. Leaving the lamp on, she went quickly down the stairs and out onto the landing, then ran lightly down the two flights of stairs to reception. Fortunately nobody saw her. She looked up and down the hall wondering where would the hotel keep buckets and cleaning stuff? Then seeing the two WC's opposite reception, she made her way to the Ladies and went in. Inside, sure enough was a toilet and behind the door a small cupboard. Opening it, she found what she was looking for, and took one of the three buckets out, and a cloth from off a pile of them on a shelf above the buckets. She closed the cupboard and pulled the main door open a notch to see if anybody was about, as she didn't want to be noticed at this stage. A guest carrying a bucket up through the hotel would be questioned. The hotel hall was still empty and quiet. She ran across and returned to the door to the attic. With her hand on the handle, the door to the Sutherland Suite started to open. Diane flung open the attic door and closed it quietly behind her. Hannah, the housekeeper, came out of the Sutherland Suite with a puzzled look on her face. Had she heard somebody? Shaking her head, decided that she hadn't and made her way along to the Caithness Suite, she was really pleased with the cleanliness of the rooms. The white glove test had found no dust at all, not like the last cleaner the hotel had employed.

Behind the attic door, Diane stood shaking, she had got away with it, now for the difficult bit. She took a deep breath and made her way slowly up the stairs to the attic. She switched the lava lamp off, and taking the cloth out of the bucket, turned the lamp upside down and unscrewed the base, then carefully she tipped the contents into the bucket. Now she just needed to wait.

Twenty minutes later, after the wax had hardened at the base of the bucket, Diane poured the liquid back into the lamp and stood it on the floor upside down with the base beside it. She turned the bucket upside down and the wax disc fell out into her hands. It was heavy, but would it be heavy enough she wondered to herself? She weighed it in her hand, it seemed heavy, ah, well, she would just have to see. Her eyes ran around the room to see if anything else came to hand, but nothing did. Diane unplugged the lamp and placed it back in the shadows. She went down and out onto the landing, closing the attic door slowly behind her. She returned to her suite, where she flung the door closed and stretched out on the bed. This was getting serious, a bit of blackmail was one thing, but murder was quite another.. Maybe she needed to think about Burgess in a different light. Maybe the blackmail note was a mistake. He was the sort of person who might just take the law into his own hands.

CHAPTER 15

Her alarm clock woke Diane who looked at the clock. She got up and went and freshened up before returning to the attic to meet Sarah who was already there waiting for her.

"I was about to go."

"Yes, sorry about that. I don't think that this is a case for the police, we don't know who it's from, or if it's real or just fiction."

"I don't think it is fiction, it is addressed to one of the guests."

"But we don't know when it was written do we? I mean it could have been written and brought here, and dropped out of a handbag or pocket couldn't it?" Diane looked at Sarah, would she believe her, or.. Sarah looked up from the chair at Diane.

"There is something else I have learnt."

"And that is?"

"You, you wrote this and are trying to blackmail Mr Burgess aren't you?"

"Me?" Laughed Diane. "Whatever gave you that idea?"

"Ms Sutherland says it was you who asked for it to be delivered to Mr Burgess, and you gave her ten shillings for it." With a roar, Diane moved fast towards Sarah, who had now risen from the chair, and was moving towards the stairs. Diana grabbed the bucket and swung it at Sarah, who ducked. The momentum took the bucket past her head and round towards Diane. Who had quickly moved and this time made a second swing at Sarah, who had turned and started to go down the top step. The bucket caught her head with a bang. Collapsing, she fell towards the door at the bottom of the stairs. Diane took the wax disc out of the bucket and quickly went down the stairs and brought the wax down hard on Sarah's head, shattering in the process. She stood above her and looked down as Sarah drew her last breath. Damn, that wasn't how this was supposed to end. She bent down and taking hold, dragged Sarah up the stairs and over to the corner of the attic, going back for the bucket. She dropped the bits of wax back into it and took the cloth and went over to Sarah to wipe away any remaining blood and then she went and broke up the pieces into smaller bits. The wax now went back into the lamp and she put it right back in the darkest part of the attic. Taking some of the boxes she re-arranged them to conceal the body and it wasn't really noticeable. Looking around for a last time, was there anything she had missed? Then noticing a small metal skylight, she reached up and twisted the handle to open it slightly. That would take any smell away and she would be long gone before the body was discovered. Just to make really sure, she took the cloth and bucket, and with the cloth in her hand, reached up and removed the light bulb, shook it and then replaced it, as hoped, the bulb had broken with the shaking while hot. She went down the stairs and carefully opened the door a crack to see if anybody was outside, no, so she left and switched out the light behind her. Anybody entering the attic now would think the bulb had blown and probably go and get a new one. She returned the bucket and cloth where she had found them along with the key. Hopefully the receptionist would just think that Sarah had gone home after finishing work.

+

The following morning, Ronald had been surprised to find a new note under his door.

Mr Burgess, I have had change of heart, maybe you would like to discuss investing a regular amount into a new money making scheme I know of. It is quite legal, say you put £10 per month in, after 10 years it has grown to £5000 pounds, now after 10 years you get to keep a quarter, which is more than you put in and I keep quite quiet about what I saw you did.You don't hear from me again, just keep paying the £10 each month as mentioned before. Not blackmail, but an opportunity to get a bit more back for you.

Ronald scratched his head and went and sat down at the desk. Reaching into the drawer, he took out a pen and paper and worked out the sums. After ten years he would be just £50 better off, but and it was a big but, he would be left in peace. He quickly penned a reply enclosed a £10 note and sealed the envelope before taking it down to reception to be delivered as addressed to the Dornoch Post Office.

+

Early that morning Bill and Jane had left the hotel and caught the train to Inverness, Bill was reading that morning paper, and Jane was sat with her head against his, as the train wound its way south. They had already been through Tain and now were approaching Invergordon.

"Happy?" Asked Bill, as the train stopped at the station.

"A bit more than yesterday."

"You were the one who wanted to go for the walk, if I recall."

"Yes, that was nice and so was the meal, but I was thinking of the two deaths at the hotel. That wasn't so nice."

"No, but that was back there, we are heading to an exhibition and a new hotel in Inverness."

"Yes, but we need to find somewhere first."

"Done that." Said Bill with a smile.

"What, how?"

"Reception offered to give me some names, and then once I had picked one, they phoned and booked."

"Aren't you the clever one." She ruffled his hair and settled back to enjoy the rest of the journey.

CHAPTER 16

Four days later Bill and Jane were walking by the river in Inverness, hand in hand. They had been real tourists, done the exhibition, gone for a boat ride down Loch Ness, and were now coming to the end of the holiday. Tomorrow they would be travelling back to home and then work after that. As they walked along the river Bill spotted a newspaper board.

"Look at that heading."

missing person not found after five days.

Police ask for help in finding her.

"That may be our hotel." Said Bill.

"Unlikely, it says missing, not dead. we can't help them, look don't let's spoil our final day." Replied Jane.

"Ok, what do you want to do then?" They had reached the Cathedral and stood on the corner of the street looking up at it.

"Bill."

"Yes?"

"You'll think me odd, but there is only one life, would you marry me?"

"What did you say?"

"You heard; will you marry me?"

"Yes, of course I will." Bill reached his arms around her and brought her towards him, and they kissed for a long time.

+

Diane had left the hotel on the same day as Bill and Jane had,

and now was staying in the very small bed and breakfast in Dornoch that overlooked the Cathedral. Her room was in the front and she had paid extra for that but gave her a clear view of the churchyard and across to the Court-house and Jail. All morning, workmen had been planting trees on the green in the front of the cathedral, and she wondered what they would look like in twenty or so years. She had been taking stock of her position since the killings in the hotel. Her first thoughts had been to get away as far as possible, but then rational thought kicked in. She decided that the last place anybody would look for her would be ten miles down the road. Dornoch was the centre of the administration of Sutherland. It had all the usual trappings as well. She had worked out with the regular amounts going into her various accounts, she could just about afford to live in Dornoch. Though finding a property that she could afford would be a bit more challenging. She could sell up her own house but was a bit reluctant to do that yet. Wait and see, that was her decision. She had already been to the Post Office in the square opposite the garage and collected the first of the 'investments' that Mr Burgess would be making for the next five years. The other men had come through with their payments, so all in all, she had a regular £100 a month coming in and being a careful woman had invested some in various banks and organizations to let it grow over time. Diane decided that life was good at the moment. If she got herself a small job, she would become a nobody, who would not be paid any attention to in this part of Scotland.

+

Flora was talking impatiently to the manager, as to why Sarah hadn't showed up for work as usual.

"Look, she is a good worker, and never has been late or missed a shift, For the first day, I thought she may have gone home, she was very upset about the death of Sidney, that I do know. Now though, it is a week, and nobody has seen any sight of her. The last time anybody saw her was entering the library, and I have been up there for a quick look and nothing is out of place."

"Calm down, you know that that sort of work is seasonal, and people come and go all the time. She was upset, you said so yourself, maybe she just needs some time to reflect and she'll come back I am sure of that. We've told the Police, but they said that as she was adult, they couldn't do anything until three days had passed. As you said, it's been a week, so now let's move on, I suggest we place an advert in *The Northern Times* and get a new person."

"Ok, maybe you are right, but I am still concerned about her." She turned and went back to her desk.

CHAPTER 17

Headington Oxford 1990

Ronald sat in his sitting room, life was good, he had paid the monthly money for the ten years. Surprisingly he had got the agreed amount back. For two years after that, he had been worried, but nothing had been forth coming. Now fifteen years on, he was relaxed. It appeared that the blackmailer had kept their word. He was still annoyed that he had been done out of a decent return and swore that one day if he ever found out who it really was, would demand his share of the real returns promised. He wasn't to know that the scheme outlined, didn't exist, and the real return was only a bit more than he had got back.

Maybe, he thought to himself, a return trip to Scotland, after all he hadn't been back in twenty five years. He reached for the phone beside his chair..

+

In Dornoch, Diane sat in the flat overlooking the Cathedral, she was content, she had regular work, in the library, and her long investments, well most of them, were still paying her every month. One or two had died or stopped, but she wasn't bothered. Occasionally, over the last twenty years, she had made one or two new means of getting money, but the old and tried methods worked the best. Careful to avoid bringing any attention of her other activities, she always went to the Borders or Northumberland to get any new foolish men. She had planned and schemed for most of her life and now had a nice flat over a bank that was paid for and money in the same bank as investment. A small, but nifty, Merc 280 convertible sat on the road, waiting for her next ride. She had kept her word and returned the money back to Burgess, it was more the making them worry for ten years that gave her a warm thrill.

+

Bill and Jane were walking along the Thames, they had married, and both now worked full-time in London. Tired but happy, they had looked forward to a return to Scotland, and to The Grand East Sutherland Hotel. Jane had said that twenty five years was more than enough time to put ghosts to bed, and they had a new car to drive in this time.

CHAPTER 18

Three months later, Bill turned the car into the drive beside a new notice-board welcoming visitors to: THE EAST SUTHERLAND HOTEL. He pulled the car into a space and nudged Jane.

"Well, here we are, they seem keen to emphasis the east Sutherland bit don't you think?" Jane looked at the entrance, above the door, in neon lights were the words "Welcome to THE EAST SUTHERLAND HOTEL".

"Well, you can't miss it, can you? Though the word Grand is missing."

"I hadn't noticed that. Well, well. I wonder what other changes we will find inside. Come on." He got out of the car and opened the boot to take out the two cases. "Don't recall having this much luggage last time."

"We were a lot younger then." replied Jane, as she reached in for her hand-bag. Leading the way, she walked up the ramp and into the hall.

Inside a long mirror hung in the stairwell, twisting one way and then back. The walls were covered with glass boxes containing everything from model toys to stuffed animals. Paintings hung off the railings of the stairs. The floor was still marble, and the games room was now a TV room. The reception area was now part of the hall, and a large sign at the back flashed on and off saying BAR. Jane looked up and saw that the stairs stopped being hung with pictures after the first floor. Nobody at reception and no bell to ring. She turned to Bill.

"It hasn't improved with age, where is the receptionist?" She banged the counter, and head appeared above the counter, followed by the rest of the woman.

"Yes?"

"We've booked a room, can you show us which one please?"

"Name?"

"Dawson." She looked at the pair of them and then turned to the computer sat on the side.

"How do you spell that?"

"D A W S O N." Sighed Bill.

"Ok, don't get shirty." We have a new suite for you both, it's on the first floor. It's one of the new ones, 'Balblair' we are redesigning the hotel, up to date changes. It's what customers want isn't it? Now just sign where I have put the X's and put your car reg number in the space provided." She pointed to the four sheets of paper. Bill signed as Jane looked around.

"First Floor did you say?" She asked.

"That's right love, it is on the left as you go up the stairs. You can't miss it, there should be a name on all the doors. Here is your key." She passed over a single key to Bill.

"Just one?"

"If you want a second one, then there is a deposit of £50.00 we can't be too careful these days."

"One will do." Bill grabbed the key and taking one of the suitcases, started to walk towards the stairs, Jane took the other and started to follow him.

"Will you be wanting Dinner tonight?" The receptionist shouted after them. Bill turned and shouted back.

"Don't know yet." Then turned and continued up the stairs. At the landing he turned to the left and found himself outside an oak door with a sign saying, 'OLD POULTNEY'. He put the key in the door, and tried to turn the key, nothing happened.

"Didn't she say Balblair?"

"On the left, first floor, she said." Jane walked along the landing, the door on the other side said 'BALBLAIR'.

"Try this door." Bill walked over and tried the key. It turned smoothly. He opened the door and let Jane walk in, he went back to get the suitcase outside Old Poultney suite, and then back into Balblair. Jane was still stood still looking at the room. Bill looked around and laughed. The room was painted totally black with small gold stars painted on the ceiling, around each of the very small lights that dotted the ceiling. A large mirror was on the wall at the bottom of the bed, and off the bedroom a large en-suite with jacuzzi was installed. The window looked down towards Golspie, with Dunrobin Castle about a mile away from the hotel. They looked at one another, and Jane laughed as well.

"I am not staying in this room." Jane said after she finished laughing.

"No, I agree. Stay here, I'll go and sort something out." Bill left the room and quickly went down to the receptionist, banging the desk, the woman appeared again in the same manner as before.

"Yes?"

"I'd like a different room, my wife and I don't like the black walls. Something a bit more tasteful perhaps, if you have something that is?"

"But that is our most requested room."

"That is as maybe, but it is not my or my wife's taste."

"Well, " She looked at the computer, and then turned back to Bill. "There is the Sutherland Room on the second floor. We have not got around to updating that yet, do you want to have a look?" She handed the key to Bill, who walked quickly up to the second floor. Opening the door, while it had been updated at some time, it was recognizable as the same room they had had twenty five years earlier. He put the latch up and went down to where Jane waited in Balblair.

"We can have our old room again. It looks a lot better than this, I have left the catch on the door, so I'll go down and return this key, and you can go on up to the room." She nodded, and picking up the suitcase beside her, turned and left the room, followed by Bill, who returned to the receptionist, who stood waiting.

"I'll take that one please."

"It's on the second floor you know."

"Yes, I found that out thank you."

"I'll have to get you to sign in again, then sign out from the other room." Sighing, she turned to the computer and a printer whirled somewhere below her, as a number of sheets of paper were spat out on the floor. She bent down and gathered them together, before stapling them together. She indicated to Bill where to sign. Then she turned and reached for a key, before giving it to Bill. "Here's your key."

"But you have given me that already."

"That's one of the two, the old rooms have two keys. Now do you want the key or not?" Bill reached and took it.

"Thank you." He turned and walked back up to the stairs and on to Sutherland Suite…

CHAPTER 19

Ronald pulled the car into a layby just outside of Tain. Getting out he stretched his aching legs. The road was quiet, it had been since Inverness, he could hear birds flying around, and it was generally peaceful. Walking around the layby, he got to the other side of the car, and reached down to get the map that was folded on the seat. Looking at it, Dornoch was around eight miles away, and the hotel, where he was going to stay, about fifteen miles. It was around half eleven now, deciding that lunch in Dornoch, and then drive on to the hotel sited between Golspie and Brora, would be his plan. He walked around the car, got in and started the engine to continue his drive North.

Fifteen minutes later, he pulled his car to the side of the road opposite the Cathedral and got out and locked it. The town seemed busy, a lot of people about. Ronald walked back to the restaurant that he had passed on the way in. An hour later after a very pleasant meal, he returned to his car. Unknown to him, he was being watched by Diane from her flat above the bank. Ronald got in and drove off towards Golspie and the North.

Diane sat down at her window seat, it was Ronald, she was sure of that, had he returned to find her? She chided herself for being so silly, he didn't have her address. Even if he did, then he would have called at the flat, as he had parked outside. But he had not done so, so she assumed that he was here on some other business. Relaxing, she opened the current *Northern Times* and started to read.

CHAPTER 20

In the hotel dining room, Bill and Jane had just ordered their lunch. While the dining room hadn't changed much, the wall between it and the kitchen had been taken down and as was now the fashion, the whole of the kitchen and all the working staff could be seen. Flames could be seen occasionally flaring from the large steak grill, that was front and centre of the kitchen.

"Do you like the changes they have made?" Asked Jane.

"Well, some of them, no, but the kitchen being visible, that is an improvement."

"Why?"

"You can see if anybody lets anything fall on the floor for starters, and if they are short staffed, that is obvious as well."

"Nowhere to hide you mean?"

"Exactly. I don't like the new colours they are choosing, black, ugh!"

"No, that wouldn't be my choice either, maybe we shouldn't have returned?"

"After twenty-five years, come on, that there would be changes, it was expected wasn't it? I expected changes, didn't you Jane?"

"Suppose so, but my mind had the layout and décor of our last visit."

"Well, it has changed, but outside hasn't changed that much. Want to walk up to the monument again, like last time?"

"Huh, you were worn out then and now you are twenty five years older. But if you want to try it, I'm game if you are." She grinned across the table and laughed as she saw the face that Bill gave. The waiter appeared with their food and they started to eat.

Ronald had checked in and had found his room, Clynelish, on the first floor. He was now stretched out on the bed, gazing at the ceiling full of small lights against the dark blue with white patches of cloud dotted around the ceiling. The hotel folder lay unopened on the desk, and his suitcase lay in a similar manner on the floor. He wondered to himself as to why hotels had to be so different and constantly changing. He closed his eyes and drifted off to a short and untroubled sleep.

+

Diane, having dozed, awoke worried, the rational side of her know that it was a pure coincidence that she had seen Ronald. It had given her a bit of a fright though. She decided to go and start to make some changes. Picking up her handbag, she left the flat making for the post office in the square.

+

An hour later Bill and Jane had eaten and were now walking in the grounds of the hotel. Bill looked back towards the round pile of stones that made up the Broch.

"Somethings never change, and others.." He left the sentence unfinished.

"You are thinking about what you saw when you were young at the Broch, aren't you?" She reached over and put her arm around his waist.

"Partly that, and why things change, not always for the best."

"That's life, and we only have the one life, so let's move forward."

"You are so full of wise words, where do you get them all from?"

"Books, articles." They continued walking towards the road. A man in his late fifties was walking towards them.

"Good evening, hope you enjoy your walk." he said.

"Good evening, are you staying at the hotel?" Asked Jane.

"Yes, just for a few days. Takes me away from the memories of my old job."

"Which was?" Asked Bill, only to be nudged by Jane.

"Bill, he wants to forget, didn't you just hear him say so. Honestly, sometimes you don't really listen do you?" Bill turned towards the man.

"Hello, I'm Bill and this is my wife Jane. We stayed here about twenty five years ago, it was 'The Grand East Sutherland Hotel' back then."

"We were wondering why the 'Grand' got removed from the name." Said Jane.

"Ah, now that is a tale and a half." He replied. "My name is Ian Reid, a retired fireman. Tell me, do you like the new hotel, now it's had a makeover?"

"Not really, we are staying in one of the older rooms, they have not been renovated yet. At least that is what the hotel are telling us." Bill replied.

"Well, the Grand got taken down when the old owners sold up and left. Then new owners bought it for a song, and started to redecorate, why some people do that before the invisibles are done beats me."

"The invisibles?" Said Jane.

"The invisibles, wiring, plumbing, central heating, those sorts of things. Get them right and the rest is easy, but too many folks do the decorating, the wiring doesn't get upgraded, and then one day, whoosh, the whole place goes up in flames."

"Is that what happened here then?"

"No, the original owners, had got the hotel up and running, then there were two deaths, well, that doesn't do any hotel any good does it? The numbers of people using it dropped right down. They took out adverts and all sorts of things, then a month after the deaths the smell started. They couldn't find out where it was coming from. Nobody came and stayed. The owners sold up and the new owners, dropped the word Grand from the name and started to re-decorate. Got as far as two rooms, then one night a machine, used for drying wet plaster, catches fire, the room is completely destroyed, as is the room underneath. They decide to sell the hotel and the current owners buy it and start redecorating again. The wiring is now over twenty five years, and needs a total re-wire, but that will not be happening any day soon."

"And the smell?" Queried Jane. "That still is there?"

"No, don't think so, anyway, I must be getting along, nice meeting you, perhaps we'll see each other again in the hotel?"

"Nice meeting you" Bill offered his hand, and Ian took it and shook it firmly. Then they watched Ian walk back towards the hotel entrance.

"Funny that, how the hotel changed after those deaths." Jane commented.

"Yes, but I wonder what the smell was due to."

They walked on out to the main road and crossed over, to start walking towards Golspie. Jane produced a small booklet from her handbag and showed it to Bill.

"This was in the room, we can walk to the Castle, then down the drive, and back along the shore to the hotel. It's clearly marked out and it says here it's a level path till the bit from the beach to the hotel."

CHAPTER 21

Later that night, Ian sat in the hotel Bar and nursed a small glass of whisky. He spotted Bill & Jane standing at the bar ordering their drinks. As Bill turned away from the Bar, he caught sight of Ian and saw Ian beckoned for them to join him. They walked over, holding their drinks and sat down. Ian was fingering a paperweight that lay on the windowsill, as part of a larger collection.

"There nice paperweights, we have one or two, mostly bought at table-top sales and the odd fete."

"Then I hope you have them displayed out of sunlight?" Asked Ian.

"Why?" Asked Bill.

"Why, because the sun, if they are in the sun's direction, can use it as a magnifying glass, and things can catch fire. I've seen curtains go from smouldering to suddenly burst into flames. Just because the sun has caught the paperweight and it has magnified the rays. It's mostly the clear glass that cause the fire risk." He added, seeing Jane's face. The other thing of risk is the Bubble lamp. How they ever got allowed beats me."

"Bubble Lamp?" Asked Bill.

"Yes, those lights that have bubbles going up and down."

"A Lava Lamp I think you mean." Said Jane smiling at Ian.

"Bubble Lamp or Lava Lamp, the point is they are a fire risk. You don't see as many these days thankfully." Ian took his glass and finished it. Bill stood up.

"Let me get you another?" He asked pointing at Ian's empty glass.

"That's very kind of you. It's called Mature Gracefully ." Bill got up and made his way to the bar, leaving Jane and Ian to talk. A few minutes later, he returned with the drinks, and sat down again.

"You, mentioning the bubble lamp, set me thinking. They used to have one here, when we first came here twenty five years ago. It didn't seem to work though. It was situated in the music room, before they made this into one room. Do you remember Jane?"

"Vaguely, now you mention it."

"Probably got rid of it, as a lot of folk did once the risk of fire was made known and they went out of fashion." Ian said, before taking a sip of the whisky.

CHAPTER 22

Ronald awoke feeling refreshed. He made his way down to the Bar, being a small hotel, it was pleasantly not overcrowded. He ordered a drink and then took it over to a small table with a couple of seats near a window and sat down. A man approached him and nodded at the spare chair.

"Anybody sat there?"

"No, sit down if you want. It's pleasant here, though a shame that the piano has been taken out." Said Ronald.

"You remember those days? That was some time ago friend."

"Yes, twenty five years since I last came here. There have been a lot of changes since then. Though I suppose that applies to all of us as well. Cheers." He raised his glass and the man did likewise.

"I'm here on holiday, I can recall those days as well, the hotel had only just got started then, though the death of a couple of the guests didn't help things, it has changed hands twice since then." He took a sip of his drink, then nodded again at Ronald. "I'm Thomas by the way, Thomas Swift. I came back after moving out of the area following my divorce. I had been paying to keep my affair from my wife, but the woman bled me dry. Regular payments would keep her quiet, but when the amounts went up and my employment ceased, then she told the wife, ex-wife" He corrected himself. "and the whole thing blew apart. Mitchell her name was, can't recall the first name though." He sighed and looked into his drink before finishing it and nodding at Ronald. "You want another of those?"

"No thanks, I am good at the moment. Her name wouldn't have been Ruth Mitchell would it?"

"Ruth, that it, why, I mean how, do you know her?"

"She got a lot of money from me for some scheme or other and I paid for years, but the return was not great. I got my capital back, but nothing else. I often wondered where she ended up. If I could find her, I would really try and get my hands on the return she promised if I 'invested' in her scheme."

"I'd like to do the same, but it is unlikely that we will ever find her again. Cheers." Said Thomas.

+

In Dornoch, that afternoon, Diane had been to the bank and the Post Office to arrange a small re-direction. She had invested in a development of 4 flats in the centre of Golspie. The plan had been to rent them out and make some real money. The building of the Dornoch Bridge, due to open next year, would mean that visitors needed no longer to stop in Golspie overnight as they had for so many years. All four flats stood finished but unsold. They had remained so for two years, and during this time, she had decorated and furnished one of the top ones, partly as a retreat, and partly to use as a show flat, should there be any interest in the other flats.

Diane re-entered her flat and set to packing a few items for a stay in Golspie. About half an hour later she was packed and driving along the road beside the old railway. Loch Fleet and its seals flashed by as she drove. Over the mound and on towards Golspie. Once there, she swung her car into the garage under the flats and getting out closed the garage door. Diane went up the stairs that led to the flats above. She had built the flats with the garages at ground level, this way avoiding any potential floods and giving a great view out sea. Behind the flats, going inland, was Lady Sutherland fountain Road, and the monument to the first Duke of Sutherland on the hill behind. Unlocking the door to the flat, Diane entered and sat down on the L -Shaped settee in the huge one room with its extensive lounge and kitchen. She gazed out through the panoramic windows that reached from floor to ceiling, A balcony was outside the flats with reinforced glass to protect against the wind and sea. Diane sat and thought to herself, maybe she should stop all the regular amounts. Tell them it was over, and live in peace and quiet. She would miss the risk and thrill of it, but the sight of Burgess had given her a shock. While she realised it was probably coincidence that had brought him to Dornoch, it was a bit too close for her liking. Not just yet, she decided, she would wait here for a couple of weeks, then go back to Dornoch. By which time Burgess would have gone. A friend she could trust, had seen him go into an Inn in Dornoch and that was probably where he would be staying. She got up and decided to go out. A new padlock for the garage as well as some other bits and pieces were needed. Diane left the flats, and started to walk towards Lindsay and Co, the Ironmongers in Golspie, you can get most things there, she thought to herself as she walked.

CHAPTER 23

The following day, Bill was outside the hotel walking in the grounds when a small van with a tail drop pulled into the drive and drove up to the front door. Emblazoned on the side of the van was the sentence,

Need to empty your house or declutter? Call us it is our speciality.

Two men got out of the van and made their way up the steps to the hotel. Bill looked thoughtfully at the van and wondered why a clearance business would be visiting a hotel, during the high season at that as a well?

Inside the hotel, the men were waiting at reception. One pressed the bell on the desk, and the other looked around the inside of the hotel.

"Yes?" Asked the receptionist crossly.

"Miss Eva Fleming? You have some stuff to be cleared? You did call us?"

"Yes, the stuff is in the attic, and needs emptying. When we took over the hotel there was an inventor, which said unused items in attic. We have not been in the attic space yet. Please can you go and clear it for us. It's entrance on the second floor. We don't have a lift, it's the stairs or nothing." She smiled and retreated to her office. The two men looked at one another, and both made for the stairs..

..Ten minutes later, they stood on the landing to the left were Sutherland, Shetland and to the right, Caithness and Orkney rooms. Doors stood between the various rooms, which on closer examination, proved to be just cupboards. No other doorway or entrance was visible to the two men. They returned to the reception and once again hit the bell.

"Yes? You again, I told you it's on the.." She was stopped in mid-sentence.

"You told us that, but we have been up there and there is no door or stairway to an attic. Now if you are wasting our time, then.."

"No, no, there must be an entrance somewhere. Let me come back up with you." She came out from the office and walked towards the stairs, the two men following her upwards.

At the top of the stairs, she looked around and went to the two cupboard doors first, then, opened the room doors and looked inside. She withdrew her head from the last room and wandered back to the two men who now had reached the landing.

"There has to be an attic entrance here somewhere. Why don't you carry on looking, and I'll go and ask somebody who may know what happened?" She turned and retraced her steps down to reception. Walking quickly to the Managers office, she knocked and entered.

"Do you have a minute to spare?"

"Why?" Asked the Manager as she looked up at Eva.

"The house clearance firm is here to clear the attic, but there appears to be no entrance to the attic, well not that they can see anyway. Do you know of anybody who would know where that entrance may be?"

"This is probably before my time, let's look at the records of the hotel." She rose and walked over to a row of large books, and ran her finger along the various books, each one being dated with five year intervals. "Now we bought the hotel three, no four years ago, so if we go back to nineteen seventy, there was a small fire then. Look, here it is." She took the book down and opened it on her desk. At the back of the book a large folded plan of the hotel was tucked into the book. Taking it out, she unfolded it and spread it across the desk. "Look, the door is between Sutherland and Caithness rooms. At least it should be there, if it isn't then they will need to come back another time when it's been found."

"Thanks." Replied Eva as she turned and left the Managers office.

Once at the top again, and now getting a bit puffed, she told the two men where it was on the plans. They all looked at the wall that was between the two rooms and saw no door at all. Eva turned to the two men.

"Look, I am sorry to have wasted your time, but can you come back once we have found a way up there please?"

"Ok, but we will have to charge you for today."

"Fine, whatever." She waved her hand impatiently at them. Looking at the wall, she shook her head and followed them down to her office on the ground floor.

CHAPTER 24

The following day saw Bill and Jane awoken to the noise of drilling nearby.

"What the..?" Exclaimed Bill as he got out of bed. "I'm not putting up with this noise at.." He stopped and looked at his watch, "Eight in the morning, in a high quality hotel."

"Bill?"

"Yes"

"We are both awake now, so why don't we just get up and go and get some breakfast, maybe we can find out just what is going on."

Bill looked at her and smiled. "Ok, let's do that." He turned and went to the bathroom to shave and shower. After ten minutes he had finished and now Jane entered to use them as he got dressed. She called out to him.

"Bill, you go down and grab a table, get me an orange juice and coffee and I'll join you in. few minutes. See if you can find out what is going on as well."

Ten minutes later Bill was sat at a table reading the newspaper. Jane walked up and sat down beside him. She tapped the paper, and he looked over the top, and then folded and placed it beside them both.

"So, what did you find out?"

"They have lost an entrance to the attic. There was a door and stairs between our two rooms back in the sixties, but at some point that has been removed. They are busy 'renovating' the other suites and are looking for the stairs to the attic at the same time, as Workmen start early, we get woken early. The management have offered to give us a bit of compensation for the disturbance though. Can you remember any stairs being there? I can't."

"I can't either, come on, let's have breakfast before it all gets eaten."

In the old Caithness suite, two workmen were busy, one drilling and the other one, getting tiles off the en-suite and bagging them as they did so. Dust lay across the room, the sunlight showing it as they worked. Eva stood just inside the room, watching at a distance. Small holes were on each of the walls, but no sign of the door to the attic. Turning, she left the room and went downstairs to her office. She was cross on two counts, one, the attic entrance didn't exist, and two the cost of the work being done in the high season, was, with the high compensation, going to be very expensive to the hotel.

Ian stood at the bottom of the stairs and looked up through the hotel to the top floor, where the noise came from. He decided to take a walk. He had overhead other guests saying the hotel were looking for an entrance that nobody knew about. He would go and talk to some people in the village, maybe somebody would know what was happening, or failing that, the local paper may be another avenue for information.

CHAPTER 25

Ronald paid for the fuel then drove away from the square and towards the bank. Parking where he had before. Luckily there was a space outside the bank. He locked his car, one couldn't be too careful and made his way to the stores he had seen on the way in.

Diane had driven over to Dornoch forgetting to pack some tins of food. Rather than buying more she had decided to return and get the ones she had in her Dornoch flat. Annoyed that she was unable to park outside the flat, she parked in front of the Cathedral, and walked across to the flat. It was just unfortunate that at the same moment, Ronald was crossing the road to his car and couldn't fail to notice Diane. Taking a second look, he realised that it was her. She had changed a bit, but not too much. He got in the car, he was shaking with the shock of seeing her and waited. Failing to notice him, Diane carried on crossing over and walked up to the entrance to the flat and unlocked the door and entered. So, thought Ronald to himself, this is where she has been hiding, I'll come back with Mr Swift, and we'll both confront her. Happy now, he switched on the engine and drove off in the direction of Golspie.

Diane, unaware that she had been seen, collected her tins of food before locking up and droving back to Golspie. She was completely unaware of just how close to Ronald and Thomas she was.

+

At the same time, Ian was talking in the Golspie Arms Hotel to a man who had been a fireman as well. He was telling Ian how the fire at The Grand East Sutherland Hotel had been put out. The owners had chosen to have the rooms redecorated, and in the process, had boarded up the entrance to the attic. The fire had started, as so many did, by overuse of an electrical adaptor. Ian had seen too many fires start that way. If he had his way, they would be banned. Ian offered the man another drink and then after a short while walked on through Golspie to the station. He wanted to see how often trains ran to Inverness.

+

Meanwhile Bill and Jane were out driving towards Brora. They had decided that a short run out to the next couple of villages may be a change of scene for them both. Having heard that La Mirage restaurant in Helmsdale was famous for its seafood, they had ordered ahead the previous day for 'the special'. As both of them loved seafood, they were looking forward to this occasion. As Bill drove, Jane turned towards him.

"Stop at Brora on the way back?"

"Ok, but we need to fill up first, doubt there is enough to get us there and back to the hotel." He drove on, and shortly came to a couple of garages, one on each side of the road. Pulling off, he stopped and refilled while Jane went and paid. They set off again and within half an hour they had arrived in Helmsdale. Parking in the centre, near the bridge both got out and sniffed, the satisfying smell of the salt sea with the sound of seagulls screeching and wheeling overhead was a heady mix, reminding them both that they were supposed to be on holiday.

"I used to associate this sound and smell with Cornwell, when I was growing up." Said Jane.

"Cornwall doesn't have the exclusive smell or sound of the sea you know." Laughed Bill, "Come on, we had better find this haven of Seafood." Taking her hand, they strolled along the street, and into La Mirage.

+

Two hours later they stepped back out onto the street, both having had an excellent meal. Now they needed to walk it off, before driving again. They walked down to the river, and along it, towards the sea.

"That was a meal and a half." Said Jane with a contented smile on her face. Bill stopped and looked at her, then nodded his agreement as they walked down to the harbour.

+

That evening, Ronald went down to the Bar and ordered his usual drink. That afternoon, he had asked the reception to leave a message for Mr Swift to meet him that evening in the Bar. Now he sat and waited while swirling a nice malt whisky in his hand, in between the gentle sips that he was taking. He noted the Bar was not as busy as previous occasions, but had also realised that the TV Room, when he passed it earlier, had been full of people watching a football match. It suited his needs that there wouldn't be as many people around to hear what he was going to propose to Thomas.

+

Eva, in reception, was fuming, the workmen had been busy drilling and breaking the rooms, ready for the new interiors, but still hadn't found any entrance to the attic. She was beginning to wonder if it really existed. She had contacted the house clearance firm and told them not to return until she found the attic. Gathering some papers together, she filed them in the correct folder, and then switched off the lights, and put the 'reception is unmanned at present' notice on the desk before leaving the hotel for the night.

+

Bill and Jane sat in the Bar with their drinks. Sat at the table next to theirs was Ronald, and he hardly glanced in their direction. Thomas entered the Bar and saw Ronald. He made his way over to join him.

"What do you want to drink?" Asked Ronald, as he stood to go to the bar again.

"Myself, I'll have a Pint of 'Old Gorse', it has a distinct flavour of its own." Replied Thomas. "Now what did you want to tell me?" Ronald brought the drinks over and set them down carefully on the table.

"Did you really mean it, when you said you wanted to find Ruth?"

"Of course, I did, why have you some news about her whereabouts?"

Ronald took a sip of his drink to savour the moment.

"Better than that, I know where she is living." He watched Thomas's face as he registered what he had just said.

"What! You actually know where to find her? Really? How far away do we have to travel."

"Twelve or thirteen miles. She is living in Dornoch."

"Dornoch! That is where I have to send the money."

"Post Office?"

"Yes! You the same?"

"Used to. Now it happened that it was quite by chance that I found out, I saw her going in her front door."

"And you know for certain that is the address?"

"We can check it on the electoral roll in the library in Dornoch can't we? But yes, I am ninety nine percent certain that is the right place. What say you, that we go there tomorrow morning, say around ten o'clock?" Asked Ronald.

"Try and keep me away, I'll see you in Dornoch, where exactly?"

"Outside the Cathedral I'll park at the South Side. and wait on the benches by the green. I'll see you there." Both men stopped and drank, one more deeply than the other, before finishing and leaving the Bar.

+

Bill looked at Jane and smiled. She hadn't paid any attention to him, but instead had been listening to the two men talking.

"Another drink?" She looked up as he spoke.

"No thanks, can we go out into the grounds for a walk?"

"Of course." He picked up his drink and finished it, then they left the Bar. Once outside, she turned to him. Bill stopped and they sat down on a nearby bench.

"What is bothering you?" He asked. "You were listening weren't you?"

"I couldn't help it, they were hardly whispering. They obviously are going to do some harm to a lady in Dornoch, don't you think the police should be told?"

"Told what exactly? That two men are going to do some harm to a lady in Dornoch, but we don't know the name of the person or the men?" Jane looked a bit crestfallen, as what he said made sense.

"We could follow them tomorrow morning, couldn't we?"

"No, we are on holiday, not following men or rescuing ladies, if they need help they will do that themselves."

"Suppose you are right, but is it interesting isn't it?"

"You are just nosey."

"Not nosey, just interested." They got up and walked on in the gardens.

CHAPTER 26

The builders had found the stairs to the attic. The hotel management had been told, and Eva was driving to the hotel to see what had happened. In the meantime, work had stopped.

Twenty minutes later, Eva briskly walked up the staircase to where the hole was. Now she could see for herself the hole in the wall, bending down she peered through, but could see nothing. Standing up, she turned to the workmen.

"Do either of you have a torch handy?"

"I've got one in the van. Wait here and I'll go and get it." Suiting the action to the word, he set off down the staircase. A few minutes later he returned with the Manager following him. He passed the torch to Eva and she held it up to the hole and bent down and peered in.

"What do you see?

"Steps going upwards."

"The old attic entrance?" He guessed.

"Looks that way."

"Look Eva, do you want us to continue with the Caithness renovations or take this wall down?" Asked one of the two builders.

"Well, we don't want dust everywhere, so can this be screened off in some way before you start to stop any dust?" The two men moved out and one took a tape measure and set about measuring the landing and the area around the hidden doorway.

"It can be done, but this side of the stairs would be out of use by the guests if that is possible?"

"I think so, don't you Eva?" Asked the Manager

"Probably, I'll need to see the register, and who is staying where first though." She swept a hand back through her hair, and thought to herself, just another problem to add to the many already on her plate. "You may as well get started by clearing this bit of the landing first though and take up the carpet and take down the curtains around this area first please." She turned and walked down the stairway to reception. The two builders looked at the Manager.

"You heard her, that way we don't get a huge cleaning bill as well." Turning, left the two men to start working again.

+

Two hours later, sheets of ply had been put up around the doorway, and a hole had been made in the wall large enough to get through. The news of the damage had soon spread around the guests and a few had tried to see what was going on, but with the ply hiding anything else, they soon gave up. Bill and Jane, being the nearest, had been offered another suite, but had turned this offer down, and were now in the dining room having breakfast.

"Less musical than the piano isn't it?" Asked Jane with a laugh as she buttered her toast.

"A lot less. Can you pass the marmalade once you have finished with it please?"

"Wonder if they will find anything exciting up there?"

"Probably a few cobwebs and the odd mouse." Bill replied.

Cobwebs were in abundance, as the first builder climbed through the opening and found a flight of stairs in front of him. A light switch was on the left, and he switched it on, but nothing happened. He turned and climbed back out.

"Going to need a few bright lights, the electric doesn't work. You got the torch?"

"No, the lady kept it."

"It wouldn't have been bright enough anyhow. We'll go back to the yard and get the spotlights. Come on." He led the way down the winding stairway and out to the lorry..

+

An hour later, they had returned with spotlights, a transformer and a long extension lead. Armed with some lights, they both climbed back through and up the stairs, the lights now illuminating the whole of the attic. Once at the top of the stairs, they placed a set of lights down carefully one at the end of the attic, boxes trunks and chairs were scattered through the attic. At one end there was scorched timber, but no other bits and pieces, it looked as though anything at that end had been quickly pushed towards the other end. One of them forced his way past the furniture and boxes letting the light flood in to the corner of the attic, where a skeleton was propped up.

CHAPTER 27

DI Gray was seated at his desk in the office and taken his first cup of coffee for the day. Relaxed, he knew that, by in large, East Sutherland was a quiet place compared to Glasgow or Edinburgh where he had heard that it was full on. No, he thought to himself, life was good. There was the occasional bit of trouble, usually around Gala weeks. He bent down and picked the first file off the top of a small pile on his desk. He started reading about the theft of a bike from outside the Golspie Post Office. The local police wanted to know if they should take it seriously. Flipping heck, he thought, must I do everything for them. He marked the file with a blue crayon, and wrote a smart note about using their brains. Then placed it in his 'Out tray'. Sighing, he reached out and picked up the next one, this was going to be a long day of paperwork he thought to himself.

Next door, DS Cooper had just answered the phone, the message sounded garbled to his ears.

"Can you slow down and repeat that please?"

"There is a body in the attic of The East Sutherland Hotel"

"A body?"

"Yes, we think you should come and take a look." With that the person hung up. DS Cooper thought to himself, The East Sutherland Hotel, that was where the two deaths had occurred all those years ago. Rising from the desk, he went down the corridor to the files room and after twenty minutes, returned and went and knocked on the door of DI Gray.

" Come in." Cooper went in and closed the door after him. "What is it, I have paperwork to go through."

"Yes Sir, but I thought you might want to take a look at a body that has been reported as being found in an attic of The East Sutherland Hotel."

"Wasn't that the place that.."

"Yes, the two deaths that back in 1965. I pulled the files." He offered them across the desk to Gray.

"Sit down a minute while I refresh myself with the facts." Gray leaned back in his chair and opened the first one. After scanning the covering page, he put it down and scanned the second file, again that was quickly read, and then he looked across at Cooper.

"A body you say?"

"Yes Sir, a body."

"Well then, we had better take a look at this body, give the Doc a call, and tell him to meet us there. Well, well, who would have thought it. Finding a body in the hotel." He rose and walked towards the door, with Cooper following him out of the building.

+

A short while later, both men were in the attic. The Doctor had taken a look and with a smile declared her dead. He would examine the skeleton in the local hospital tomorrow morning at 8.00am. He had then left the two policemen and Eva in the attic.

"Well Sir, what do you think?" Asked Cooper.

"I think that we have a murder on our hands, a Sutherland Murder to be precise."

"Murder!" Shouted Eva, the echo reverberating around the attic.

"Yes, murder, and don't tell the world. In fact, please can you go downstairs and wait to be spoken to later. In the meantime, not a word to anybody, understand?"

"Yes Sir." Eva left the attic and they could hear her feet clattering down the stairs.

"Well, it didn't curl up and die there. Look there is a nasty dent in the skull. I am more interested in why the body was never found before. Surely somebody must have been up here in since she was killed. They would have seen her wouldn't they?"

"Not really Sir, if you take away the lights, and just use a standard 40watt lamp that is in the middle of the room, then that light would not really shine back here, and there was a lot of boxes and stuff pushed to this side of the attic, at least that is what the workmen said."

"Just lucky then?"

"Good luck played a part, and some nerve too, leaving a body up here. Wonder why nobody reported anybody missing at the time?"

"Good question. Add that to the why she was left undisturbed for so long. We have a real investigation on our hands. I'll need to go and clear this with high ups and get some extra staff, this will be too big for us alone." Said Gray.

"Shall I interview the guests and staff?"

"The guests, I doubt that any of the current guests will have been here whenever she was killed. You would be better asking for the longest serving staff member. They may remember something about a member of staff going missing."

"Why staff?"

"Do you really think that a guest would come up here."

"Right you are, I'll seal this as well." He watched as Gray left and walked down the stairs to the hotel, leaving him alone in the attic. He flashed the torch around and tried to imagine what went on the last time the person had come up here. He sighed, they would need to empty the attic and go through all the boxes and items up here. Best to start making a list, he pulled out his notebook and started writing.

+

Downstairs the two builders sat in their van, neither of them speaking at present, they had been too shaken by the finding of the body.

+

Eva sat at her desk, wondering who the person was that they had found. she knew that this meant the end of the season. The hotel would be closed for the police. It would be doubtful that anybody would want to come and stay. She wanted to learn more but knew that to ask would lead to more questions about her and the background.

CHAPTER 28

Diane stood in her kitchen looking up at the Ben. She heard a police siren go by but didn't pay much attention Then a second and third one could be heard approaching. She stopped daydreaming and looked down at the main road. A black van and another police car were both driving north. Whatever was going on, it was either a large traffic accident or something else? Diane watched the road, if it was a road accident, then there would not be any traffic on the road going south. After a few minutes she had seen quite a bit of traffic and had realised it must be something else. Diane decided to phone the local paper see if they knew anything.

"Northern Times."

"Hello Northern Times, do you know what is going on, as have just seen a load of police cars and vans driving north."

"No idea, but we'll look into it. Thanks for phoning." They hung up. Diane put the phone down and tapped her fingers on the kitchen surface top. Maybe she would go for a drive north herself, see what was going on." She left the kitchen and went down to the garage to get her car.

+

In Dornoch, Ronald and Thomas stood looking up at the flat above the bank. They had been to the library, and found the only person on the electoral roll was a Mrs Diane Bird. That was all they had found out so far, and having knocked the door twice to no answer, now wondered what they should do next.

"I tell you that it is her." Said Ronald. "A bit older, I accept, but it is still her."

"Ok, let's say it is, but she is not here now, is she?" Ian thought for a minute, "Wonder if she had seen you and taken flight?"

"Oh, come on, she was getting money from us, why should she be frightened? She didn't seem the sort of person who would be frightened off easily."

"Suppose not. Maybe she is shopping."

"Ok, let's split up and go and look in the shops, if either of us spots her, head back here and wait in the Cathedral for the other one to turn up, then we'll take it from there."

"Sounds like a plan." The two men moved away and started to visit the shops in Dornoch.

An hour later, both men were back and seated in the Cathedral, talking in a low whisper.

"Well, did you see her anywhere, I didn't."

"Nor me, let's go and get a drink and then we will go back to the hotel. Mind you, there may not be much of a hotel there now. They were ripping a room apart the last I heard."

"And screened off part of the top landing."

+

Shortly, they both sat at the Golf Road Hotel with a drink. The bar was connected to the main dining room, and they could see the picture window overlooked the third tee of the famous Golf Course. Ian nodded towards the window.

"Maybe she is playing golf? That is what a lot of people who live in Dornoch come to do."

"Well, that can easily be found out, we ask at the course booking office." Ronald finished his drink and started to get up. A man approached them.

"Couldn't help overhearing, are you looking for somebody in Dornoch?" He asked.

"Well, yes as it happens, why do you want to know?" Asked Thomas.

"I've lived here most of my life and know most of the residents. Who is it you are wanting to find? I am Andrew, Andrew Bird." He extended a hand to them, and they both stood and shook it.

"Any relation to Diane?" Asked Ronald casually.

"My divorced wife. Is that who you are looking for?"

"Yes, do you know where she might be?" Asked Thomas.

"Well, she and I divorced some years ago now, she always kept going off on trips, without me, so we decided that we would be better apart. I have a nice flat here, overlooking the golf course, and she has got her properties Golspie and Dornoch."

"Properties, did you say?" Asked Ronald with some interest.

"Yes, a flat over the bank here in Dornoch and a set of flats she had built in Golspie, in the centre, you can't miss them, right in the centre, fantastic views out to sea and garages under them. If ever it floods again the properties wouldn't be damaged. Well, her car might, but that would be all."

"Does she live in the flats then?"

"Well if she isn't here, then, yes, you will probably find her there. Flat number one, it's the only occupied one.. Good luck finding her, and don't mention me, I try to keep out of her way these days." He left the two men looking at one another.

"Golspie! Would never had thought of going there to live." Said Thomas. "I mean it is nice enough, but given the choice, Dornoch would appeal to me."

"But he said she has both. I suppose that if she gets tired of Dornoch crowds in the summer she can go over to Golspie. It's not a far drive these days."

"Let's go and confront her, come on." Said Thomas excitedly.

"No, wait a minute. We now know where she lives, and she doesn't know that we know, we could play her game back at her."

"Blackmail you mean?"

"Yes, that is exactly what I mean. Let's go to the library and see what we can draw up and frighten the living daylights out of her." The two men left the hotel excitedly.

+

Diane had driven towards the village of Brora but had been stopped by the police at Dunrobin Castle and told to turn down the drive and return to Golspie. All traffic heading north was now being stopped and the traffic heading south was being given a choice of a very long wait or a very long diversion. She now sat in her favourite armchair and looked out across the bay in the distance. What was going on she wondered to herself. She would have to wait to find out.

+

DS Cooper had spent the last six hours, with the help of the local Crime Scene Investigators (CSI), clearing the attic. He stood in the empty space. The CSI had not found much in the attic but had found a couple of sets of prints on a lava lamp and a heavy bucket base. The skeleton had been removed. Thankful for that, he took a look around the room. The only thing of real interest had been a small earring that had been found near the top of the steps. Now bagged and in his pocket, he went down the stairs to the landing. The opening had been totally cleared. A temporary door frame and door had been installed. He locked it and sealed it with police tape. Then descended the winding staircase to the reception area where Eva would be waiting to be interviewed.

+

Bill and Jane had been told to pack and leave their rooms. They had been offered an alternative room in the hotel. The police had then decided that all the guests had to leave, unless they had been there twenty five years earlier in which case they had to stay. They now found themselves one floor down in a suite called 'Old Poultney'. It appeared that all the rooms were to be called after the various whisky firms in North. Bill threw their case on to the case stand and looked out of the two windows. One facing North and the other North West. Neither view was that great, he thought to himself. Keeping those thoughts to himself, he turned towards Jane.

"Bit better than their first offering of a room." He nodded his head around the room. Brightly lit walls with photographs of various parts of East Sutherland, a couple of easy chairs and a small writing desk furnished it. In the bedroom a four poster bed and an en-suite as well. At the window was a telescope, being currently used by Jane.

"Come and look over here Bill, you can clearly see the Broch." She beckoned him over. Bending down he took a turn at looking through it. The image was crystal clear. Standing up, he stroked his chin thoughtfully.

"Why would there be a telescope pointing at the Broch? It was pointing that way wasn't it, when we came in, I mean?"

"Yes, all I have done is to focus it. Why?"

"Well, if you wanted to see it, then most people would go and take a look, it's in the grounds after all."

"Probably. Now can we unpack our things please? I just threw things together, when they told us we had to move out." For the next ten minutes they unpacked and placed the various bits and pieces around the rooms, as one does when on holiday.

+

Outside the hotel, DI Gray and Cooper were in discussion with Eva. They had asked her to come outside as they did not want to be overheard.

"Miss Fleming, all I need to know from you is this, has anybody been looked for or asked about a missing person in the last twenty five years? Connected to the Hotel, I mean." Gray stood waiting for her answer.

"I don't really know, I have only been here a couple of years myself. You would need ask the manager. Mind you, he was not running the hotel back then. The hotel was a totally different sort of place then, or so I am told. I doubt that records are still around from those days Sir." She looked across at the Broch in the grounds.

"Do you know who might have any records of back then?" Asked Gray.

"I told you, I don't know. Maybe the local Council may have records some-where, I don't know, really I don't."

"Ok, Ok, we just want to see if we can find out who the person was. You haven't worked here very long and the hotel has changed hands. See how this now becomes a problem for us?" Said Cooper. He looked at Gray and said. "How about Companies House in Edinburgh?"

"How about them?" Replied Gray.

"They would hold records of who directors were and their addresses."

"Go to it then, you might be on to something." Gray turned to Eva, "We have finished with you for now, but might need you later, so don't leave the area without telling me or DS Cooper first. I also need a list of the current guests and their addresses If you can find out, if any of them were here twenty-five years ago that would be very helpful."

She left the two policemen wandering around the grounds.

+

Ronald and Thomas sat in the Dornoch Library. Both had been composing a number of notes to Diane, but each one had been screwed up and tossed on the floor until the librarian had brought it to their notice by bringing a bin bag over, coughing loudly. They had taken the hint and collected all the paperwork together, along with a promise to take it away when they left. Both men now had a plan on how to get Diane to return their money or the interest on it as easily as it had been taken from them.

+

Ronald had returned his hotel thinking that only himself and Thomas knew about the past dealings with Diane. As he walked up the hall, Eva called after him.

"Mr Burgess." He stopped and turned back to the reception area.

"Yes?"

"As you know the police have been called, and they want to know if any of the guests have ever stayed here before this year."

"Ronald thought for a bit, if he said no, and they found he had, then he would be caught out in the lie. If, however, he said yes, then the police would want to know what and when that was. Deciding to bend the truth a bit, he replied.

"This is my first visit to this hotel." He said, stressing the 'this' to emphasis the difference from the older Hotel. "Why, does it make a difference?"

"Only that the guests that had stayed before, can stay on. Otherwise it means, regretfully, that you will need to find another hotel or similar to stay in." She shrugged her shoulders as if to say, that is not my concern right now.

"But where do I stay? Are there any rooms in the other hotels nearby? Come to that, are there any hotels nearby?"

"A few" she replied, ticking off her fingers as she spoke. "There is The Doe Inn, and The Sit and Stay Inn, though that is a bit down market to here, The Last Tee hotel, they are all in Golspie. Then going further out, in Brora, there is, The Crows rest, The Harbour Arms, The Three Bridge hotel. In Helmsdale, there is only a couple, Stags Retreat and the Rest and be Thankful. If you go south, then Dornoch probably has the better selection, after us, that is, there is The Golf Road Hotel, but that is pricey, Jailers Rest, Sutherland Gathering Pub, or The First Hole. That last one overlooks the golf course." She stopped and looked at him.

"Do you know if the ones in Dornoch are able to take me?"

"Can't say, but I can give you the list of numbers that all the other guests have been given," She reached under the counter and produced a sheet of paper with a list of names and numbers printed on them. Eva passed it to Ronald with a smirk that seemed to say, good luck with that mate, it's the height of summer.

"Thank you." Said Ronald as he took the paper from her. "I'll give this the once over and try and find somewhere." He walked away down the hall and up to his room Clynelish. He spent the next twenty minutes checking hotels on the list, but as Eva had said, most were fully booked. The one exception so far being The Golf Road Hotel in Dornoch. They had a small suite, with a view of the course, and only a mere five hundred pounds a night. He had almost choked at that, and had said no, that was too much. He sat on the bed, the phone on the bed beside him, looking at the list, before he dialled the last one on the list. Jailers Rest.

+

Bill had been talking to Jane about the past and decided to go and walk to the Broch once more, she said that she didn't want to come, and would stay in the hotel. He set off in the direction of the Broch reflecting as he did so.

+

While in his room, between trying the various hotels around East Sutherland, the phone rang in Ronald's room and he picked up, wondering what the desk wanted now. He didn't think of anybody else that knew he was staying there, forgetting that Thomas was also staying there.

"Hello, who's there?"

"Hello Ronald, it's me Thomas, can we meet to finalise things, I have got some envelopes, I stopped on the way here, at the post office in Golspie and bought some. Thought that at the Broch might be a good place, inside there would be no way anybody could see us. Say about twenty minutes time?"

"Twenty minutes then. I'll wear a red jacket." Ronald put the phone down and got up and found a smart red jacket to put on, and then went down to go to meet Thomas.

+

Bill had got to the Broch a few minutes earlier, and stood looking up at it, before starting to walk around it and up to the top to get the best view.

Ronald got there about ten minutes later, and not seeing anybody, as Bill was on the further side of the Broch, proceeded to make his way into the centre. Thomas stood there waiting for him to arrive.

"Here are the four envelopes and each one I have put one of four and so on. That way she'll realise that more will be coming. I have addressed it to her Dornoch flat, as we are not supposed to know about the Golspie flats. If she is smart, she may have a redirection set up, if not, then she needs to go and collect the post on a regular basis, so either way, she will get it sometime." He passed the envelopes to Ronald.

+

Bill had reached the top of the Broch and after looking around at the country he glanced downwards into the centre. He felt somewhat giddy, as though a flashback to when he was ten again. The same man was there with a second man, older it was true. Forgetting he would get older. Taking another glance, just to make sure, and then quickly moved out of their line of sight. He didn't think that they had noticed him, but better to be safe than sorry. He slowly made his way around the opposite side to the entrance, and down the steeper side and back to the hotel. All the time wondering if he should tell the police what he had seen. He decided that asking for Jane's thoughts first may be a better solution.

+

Thomas was the first to leave. He made his way back to the hotel, leaving Ronald to go and post them in the village. Thomas felt that going into the Post Office again so soon after buying the envelopes may make him more memorable if asked. so Ronald could safely post them.

In the hotel, Bill was explaining to Jane how he had seen the same man again in the Broch. Like before talking to another man.

"Ok, are you sure you hadn't been dreaming? I mean the same person in the same location, but thirty six years later. What are the odds?"

"I tell you Jane, it was the same person, same place, now I doubt that there will be any blood on the grass, but should I tell the police, that is all I am asking you." He paused to get his breath back.

"Here is the problem, if you do tell the police, then they will want to know why didn't you do so back then? Are they going to believe you? It's not me you need to convince, but them. Do you know where he is staying, that would be a start."

"Presumably here." Replied Bill.

"Not necessarily, the Broch is an ancient monument, open to anybody to view, there is a car park opposite it over the other side of the main road."

"Then I'll keep my eyes peeled, and if I see him again, then make a decision at the time."

"Better, now come on downstairs to the Bar, and I'll buy you a drink."They both left the room and went down to the Bar.

+

Ronald unaware that he had been seen with Thomas. Had gone the long way to the Post Office, and had posted the first letter off to Diane, although it was posted second class, he was sure that it would get there quickly as the postman had looked at it as he took it under the glass and then put it on the small shelf behind the counter, rather than the two mail bags hanging there marked first and second. He presumed that there was some sort of local way for dealing with mail in East Sutherland. He left the Post Office and walked briskly back along the shore and up the pathway to the hotel. Ronald decided he had earned a drink and went to the Bar. As he ordered his usual drink, Bill spotted him and quietly brought this to Janes attention.

"Look, there is the man, the one at the bar, ordering his drink."

"He looks so respectable, are you sure that it is him?"

"I am certain, it is the same man." Jane leaned slightly nearer the bar, in time to hear Ronald ask for it to be put on his room account, Clynelish. She leaned back, and got up and walked towards the bar, and ordered a new round for both of them. Taking the opportunity to take a good look at Ronald as she did so. She smiled at him, and Ronald tipped his head at her, before moving to a small table at which a man was already seated. It was obvious that they knew each other, and she moved back with the drinks to Bill at their table.

"If you are correct, he is staying here, so it should be easy to check at reception, come on, take your drink with us, we can pretend we are going back to the room." She picked up her glass and took a drink from it, before rising and following Bill out into the hallway. They walked down to reception and rang the bell. Eva appeared from the office.

"Yes?"

"We were wondering, if any other guests have been told to stay in the hotel, only if it is only us, then it could be a bit," She paused, "scary?" She smiled at Eva. Who then bent down and took out a large ledger.

"We may be computerised, but the owners like to have a hard copy as well," She ran her finger down the page, and looking up, smiled at Jane. "A few people are having to stay, we have a Mr Gardner, Swift and Reid. And yourself of course. Now is there anything else you need to know?"

"No thanks." Replied Bill and watched as Eva put the ledger away before returning to the office. He took Jane by the arm and led her outside the hotel. "So now all we need to do is identify those three men, and one of them should be my man."

"If he stayed here twenty five years ago that is." Reminded Jane.

CHAPTER 29

DI Gray, seated at his desk was engrossed in the paperwork that always seemed to grow, once a case had started. The phone rang, he rummaged under the paperwork, looking for the phone, as it continued to ring. Eventually he found it on the floor, where he had put it to make more room for the paperwork. He grabbed the receiver just before it stopped.

"Yes?" He asked sharply.

"DI Gray?"

"Who wants to know?"

"It's the hotel, I have made a list of the people who were staying in the hotel about 25 years ago, and who are staying here today. I don't have the addresses though, just the names."

"Well it's a start I suppose." He rummaged around looking for some paper to write on, not finding any, he turned the report he was reading over and took a pen in his hand. "Ready when you are."

"Right, Mr and Mrs Dawson, Mr Burgess, Mr Reid, Mr Gardner and Mr Swift. You might want to know that Mr Burgess is from Oxford, the Dawson's are from London, Mr Reid is local to Golspie, and Mr Swift and Mr Gardner, they have scribbled their addresses, it looks like," She paused for a moment, "think it is New.. Something, not too clear, could be Newcastle, or Newhaven, anyhow hope that helps with your enquires." Before he could speak, she had hung up. Gray sat there for a few minutes holding the phone, and then replaced it back on the floor.

"Cooper!" He shouted, who shortly appeared at his door. "Ah, there you are, here is a list of the people who have been at the hotel on both occasions, that is, twenty-five years ago, and now." He scrambled for the list and handed it to Cooper. "Here take a photocopy and bring the original one back to me. It goes into this file I am reading."

"Right you are Sir." Taking the paper, he left the room and returned with the original, which he handed back to Gray. "I'll start trying to find their addresses?"

"Yes, yes, and find out what their employment is as well if possible."

"Right you are Sir." Cooper left the room, and Gray turned his head back towards the paperwork,

+

Diane bent down to pick up the post on her doormat. She was surprised to be getting any, other than electric and oil bills. She quickly skimmed through the small pile, sorting as she did so. This looked interesting. She went over to her desk and taking a small wrought iron letter opener, slit the top neatly and took out the letter that Thomas and Ronald had written. Diane quickly took in the gist of the letter and laughed. So, they want their money and interest back, some hope. Pouring a large glass of soda and lime, she re-read it, and noted there was no address, but, did notice that the letter had been hand stamped, meaning that it had been posted in Golspie, and yesterday as well, judging by the date on the letter. Well, well. They must be living locally, staying in a hotel or b and b? Hotel, she decided, as the two of them wouldn't have been staying together. This is interesting, as there are only a few hotels in Golspie, it wouldn't take long to find which one they were staying at. Smiling, she fetched a coat, and left the flat to walk towards the south of the village.

Ten minutes later, she had visited The Last Tee Hotel, and the Doe Inn, neither of which had heard of either Burgess or Swift, Diane was making her way towards The Sit and Stay Inn, on the way out of the village going North. She went inside and asked but got the same reply. Coming out of the front of the hotel, she glanced northwards, towards The Sutherland Inn. It looked closed and had lost some of the finesse that it had used to have. Sighing, she wandered up the road to their door, sure enough it was closed, due to staff shortages, or so the sign indicated. It looked faded and run down. Looking north, she realised that they must either be staying at The East Sutherland Hotel or could be anywhere north, west or south of Golspie. Diane did not relish a walk to the East Sutherland, so turned and went back to get her car.

+

Ronald had secured a room at Jailers Rest. He thought it was better in some respects to the last one, and certainly the staff seemed more friendly. He knew that waiting for Diane to respond was going to be hard. He wasn't the most patient kind of person. Thomas and he had agreed to wait for two days, and then if Diane hadn't responded, a second letter, posted from Dornoch, would be sent, this demanding more money as she had ignored the first one. However, all he could do now was to explore around Dornoch. While Dornoch is very nice to visit, as are most of the villages in East Sutherland, once you have completed the circuit, there is not really a lot to do, unless you play golf, something that Ronald had never had the inclination to take up.

Had he bothered to go out right away then he would have seen Diane go across the square and into the Cathedral. Had he waited to see her come out again, he would have had a long wait, as she had walked right through and out the north door, and across to her flat. She had parked in the square. She decided. in case somebody was following her, to walk via a roundabout way back to her flat. She hadn't seen anybody following her, but that was because Thomas was already watching the flat. He didn't really trust Ronald, and although working together, he decided to keep Diane under observation by himself. His reasoning was if she was seen going to the bank, then it was probable that the money would be forthcoming, if not, then there were other ways of extracting money from an unwilling person.

Ronald was now strolling around the Cathedral, and as he got close to the North Door, saw people coming out. He walked on towards the flat. Diane was at her front door, as he drew level with the bank. Thomas saw Ronald walking towards the flat, and wondered to himself, what is his game then? He sat and watched to see what would unfold.

Diane looked out through her telescope at Thomas sat on the green. She moved to the window and glanced down. seeing Ronald down at the bank. It became obvious to her, that they both knew where she lived, both here and in Golspie. Time to put things on her terms, she thought to herself, gathering up a few bits and pieces. Having put them in the car, Diane walked towards the two men.

+

Thomas went over to Ronald.

"What are you doing here?"

"I've moved out of The East Sutherland Hotel, had to, the police only wanted those people who were there twenty five years ago."

"But you said to me that you were there then."

"I was but would rather it was kept quiet."

"Ok, but I am still there, so I'll keep you up to date with what is going on, shall I?"

"If you would be so kind."

"Right, you two, what is your game?" Interrupted Diane as she got to the two of them. "Do you really think you can blackmail me?"

"Well, I am sure the police will want to listen to me, when I tell them I know who carried out the two murders in the hotel twenty five years ago." Said Ronald with a smirk on his face.

"I doubt that somehow, the police said it was accidental, on both occasions."

"Police have a habit of keeping paperwork and stuff for years and years. They'll just re-open the files. It's just a question of nudging them in the right direction, I guess." Said Thomas. The two men stood looking at Diane, wondering what or who would make the next move.

"Do your worse, I doubt that anything will come of it, look at the pair of you, silly men, who I have taken for a ride. I am well known around here, I invest in both people and business, and it is unlikely that anybody will believe you."

"So, you aren't going to give us the money or interest?" Asked Ronald.

"Got it in one." Now if you will excuse me, I have things to do." Diane left the two men and walked towards the antique shop in the square, she had helped the lady start it up years ago, a little seed money, and ever since then it had been well worth the investment.

At the East Sutherland Hotel, the house clearance van had returned. The two men had been called back by Eva, and now were busy taking boxes of bits and pieces from the hotel to the van. Bill watched from the gardens as they seemed to be constantly in and out, and the pile of items in the van was getting larger and larger. Being nosey, he wandered over to the back of the van. There wasn't much room left, not enough to stand up in, just room for three or four boxes on the floor by the rolling door. He moved out of the way as the two men returned for the last time. Bill noticed that out of the box of the last one to go in, was sticking up a lava lamp. He called out to the older of the two men.

"How much do you want for the lava lamp?"

"Huh?" Replied the man.

"This Lava Lamp." Bill picked up the lamp, and the base fell off.

"That tat? You can have that for free, its broken, the base keeps falling off, the liquid has all dried up inside as a consequence of the base being loose. It's not worth anything to me."

"Thanks." Bill scooped up the two bits of lamp and carried it into the hotel whereupon Eva, mistakenly thinking it was coming back to the hotel, ran over to him.

"No, no that is to go out with the other bits of rubbish. Oh, I am sorry, I thought you were with the property clearers."

"I'm not, but I have taken a liking to this lamp, so they have given it to me. Once it is cleaned up and working, it will be fine." He looked at the dusty lamp, and laughed, "Do you have an old box I can put this in?" Eva pointed at several lying in the hall.

"Help yourself." She turned and left Bill to it. He grabbed the nearest one, put the two bits of lamp in it and carried it out to the car, he didn't think that Jane would appreciate it if he turned up at the room with a dusty broken lamp, he thought to himself.

+

"What kept you?" Asked Jane, who had gone on ahead to the room after their walk in the grounds. "Look at you, you have dust all down the front of that shirt. Come over here, and I'll try and get it clean, no on second thoughts, take it off, and we'll get the hotel to clean it. What have you been doing to yourself? I can't leave you for five minutes can I?" Bill grinned and did as she said, then told her about the lava lamp, and how it had triggered something in his memory. What it was, he couldn't for the life of him, though think.

CHAPTER 30

DI Gray stood talking to the Doctor, he was listening as the Doctor pointed out to him the various dents in the skull of the victim, and that the person was female.

"Really, there is not a lot more I can tell you, other than it was a serious blow to the head, with something round and heavy. As to what it was, no idea, about four to five inches across. There is one thing though that might help you."

"Anything at all."

"Well, there is a small fleck of red, not sure what it is, it could be paint, but I have sent it off to the lab for them to check it out. I'll let you know as soon as I hear something."

"Red you say?"

"Red, that I am sure of."

"Ok, I'll bear that in mind. Thanks Doc." Gray turned and left the room brooding over what he had learned. Driving back to the office, he pulled in and phoned Cooper to ask if he had found anything else about the guests.

"A few of them yes, but some are proving a bit more difficult to find out about."

"Who exactly?"

: Well, Mr Burgess lives in Oxford, he was connected to the University and then retired about twenty-five or so years ago."

"And that's unusual?"

"It is when you are only in your late forties."

"Ah, that is interesting. Did he inherit any money?"

"Not that I can see so far. He seemed to have just upped and given his notice in and left and retired. Nice if you can get that sort of thing."

"Keep digging, that may be a reason for somebody to be killed, falling out over money, etc. Anybody else?"

"The couple. Bill and Jane. No police record. But can't find out any details of their lives either. Not under those names anyhow."

"I'll be over there shortly, am on the way back from the Hospital, it's a female, and a blow to the head killed her."

"There is a surprise, Sir."

"Ok, no need for that. Keep at it." The phone went dead.

+

Diane entered the antique shop. The bell rang and a lady appeared from behind a hanging curtain, that led to the stockroom at the rear. It also led to the storeroom above the property and the basement below it.

"Anything interesting today?"

"The boys aren't back yet from the hotel, give them a day to unload, and then come back. The stuff the hotel are planning to get rid of may be junk to them, it may be a gold mine to us." She smiled at Diane, who nodded and left the shop. The van drove along the road and skidded into the parking slot in. the front of the shop. Exasperated, the owner came out to the van before the driver had the chance to get out.

"Round the back, don't you listen to anything I tell you?"

"Ok." He restarted the engine and with a black belch of exhaust reversed out and along the side road to the back entrance, where a pair of tall wooden fronted gates were open and ready for the van to drive in. As soon as it was in the yard, the pair of men jumped down and quickly shut the gates. Now they could unload in peace and without being overlooked..

+

DI Gray was not enjoying that morning, first the visit to the Hospital, now at the hotel the items they had set aside to be looked at had been taken away. Now, Eva, the receptionist, was bemoaning the fate of the hotel, and the deaths, and swearing it was doomed to fail.

"Never mind all that, who has the stuff? I can go and get it, problem sorted." Eva looked at him and then laughed.

"They did us a favour once they saw the items. We didn't have to pay them, so I didn't get a receipt or anything"

"How did you hear about them then?"

"we had a flyer dropped off a few weeks ago, I kept it, and have it somewhere I think, but I need to go and clean up first." She dabbed her face and turned and left him standing in the hallway. As he stood there, a couple, obviously together, walked by, and he overheard the lady, as they did so.

…"and you kept it in the boot of the car?"

"Yes, well I didn't think you would want me to bring in a dusty lava lamp. Anyway, you.." They walked out to the car and gardens, DI Gray stood there, and then quickly caught them up as they arrived at their car.

"Excuse me, I couldn't help overhearing, Sorry, " He produced his warrant card. "DI Gray. North Highland Division. Can I take a look at the lamp, where did you get it from, the hotel?" Bill looked both at the policeman and then his wife.

"Saw it in a box of stuff that a clearance firm were bringing out to their van, thought it triggered a memory, and asked them to sell it to me, they said it was broken and I could have it free. Here it is." He bent down and took the lamp, upside down, out of the box and handed it to DI Gray. "Just be careful, the bottom is loose, the reason the contents evaporated I expect." Gray took the lamp and carefully looked inside, he could make out at the bottom, the top really, he thought to himself, a small round of wax. He passed the lamp back.

"Hold that a minute, will you please?"

"Ok." Bill took the lamp and watched as DI Gray took out a small penknife and reached down into the lamp and scraped a bit off the wax at the base, withdrawing his penknife he looked at the end of the blade and noticed it was tipped with a bit of the wax, it was coloured blue. Sighing, he looked at Bill.

"Thanks, I just needed to take a small test of the colour of the wax, we are looking for.." Stopping himself in time, he added lamely, "The murder weapon, though this is not it. Enjoy it sir, if it gets going again that is. You don't see many of them of that size nowadays do you?" And with that he went back into the hotel. Eva stood waiting and offered him a small A5 size flyer. The wording was clear and simply said they could clear from a room to a mansion, just call this number.. He jotted the number in his notebook and passed the paper back to Eva.

"You might need that again, pity there is no address. Any idea where they came from?"

"No idea, now if that is all, I have a hotel to run. There are not many guests, but still needs must." She turned and left him standing in the hall.

+

Jane looked at the lamp, and then carefully put it back in the box, and closed the boot of the car.

"You really want this thing?"

"It is reminding me of something important, so yes, until I remember, then I can get rid of it."

"Ok, as long as you do so." They walked back to the hotel and up to their room.

+

In Dornoch, the van stood empty and now three piles stood in the yard, one for junking, one for selling in the shop, and one for going to auction in Glasgow. There was a local auction house in Inverness, but that didn't get the prices that Glasgow did. The owner stood looking at the piles. She reckoned that the auction would be the profitable, the shop stuff would eventually sell. Some stuff just didn't cut it in a place like Dornoch. She picked up a lava lamp, a red one, loose base too, and looked inside, as she did so, her hand felt something rough on the base. She moved out into the light, and set it down, upside down, on a workbench. Leaving it on the workbench, she went back into the shop and returned a few minutes later armed with a magnifying glass. It was something red, and it looked like, she ran an experimental finger along it. Not wax, what then? She wondered. She picked up the lamp and carried it through to the store at the back of the shop and placed it in a wooden crate lying on the floor before putting a lid on it.. Should she tell the police, she wondered. What if it was connected to the hotel death? She would sleep on it and decide tomorrow morning what to do. For now, at least was safe enough. She had noticed though, carved into the base, was a ½ so she presumed there was another one somewhere. She would keep her eyes open for it. A pair, blood or not, always fetched more when sold together.

+

The next day, she decided that the police didn't need to be involved, it was probably years old, and may have just been blood from a cut off somebody, when they were fixing the base. She looked up as the door jangled. Diane stood there looking around and agreed with her about the best things to put to auction. Diane had noticed the lava lamp, picking it up, said that she could arrange for it to be fixed. As the 'sleeping partner' of the shop, as a rule, she didn't do much, but occasionally could repair or arrange for somebody to repair the occasional high worth item. The lava lamp had intrigued her, and she wanted to take a closer look.

Diane sat in her flat in Dornoch, in front of her was the lava lamp, still in the box that it had been in at the shop. Her eye had seen the base was loose, and there was a ½ on the base. Two would be worth much more, she thought to herself, pity there was only one of them, she mused to herself, they had come from the hotel, maybe the other one was still at the hotel. Grabbing her car keys, she left the flat and drove off towards the hotel.

+

Eva, had just about had enough, first the police had been in the attic. Then they had piled the items from the attic in a heap on the landing. Now that she had got rid of it all. Then DI Gray phoning and said he wanted to check something and not to get rid of anything else. She looked up as a lady approached the desk.

"Can I help you?"

"I hope so, I collect Lava Lamps, and wondered if you had any you didn't need any longer? I would be quite willing to pay for them." Eva looked surprised and a bit taken back.

"We did have some, but they were taken away by a clearance company, only yesterday as it happens, you are the second person to want to know who took them."

"The second?" Diane wondering who the other person was.

"Yes, the local police want to re-examine the items, don't know why, as it was all out of the attic, and had been up there for years collecting dust."

"The attic you say. Is there anything else up there?"

"Not now, there was loads, but it is cleared now. Now is there anything else I can help you with?"

"No, nothing at the moment thank you." Diane turned and left the hotel. Badly shaken by the knowledge that the attic had been cleared. She wondered if they had found the body yet? There had not been anything as far as she was aware, but then she didn't really read the papers much just *The Northern Times* on a Thursday night or Friday morning. She would have been even more concerned if she had been alert enough to spot DI Gray walking into the hotel as she left it.

DI Gray, stood in the attic, looking at the corner where the body had been discovered. Apart from a blow to the head, nothing else had been learnt. The feeling that something was missing, kept niggling him. The attic was totally clear now giving him a lot more light to see by. The items that had been stored here were now all gone. According to Eva Fleming a house clearance firm had done what they said, cleared it away. Too bad, he thought as he took a last look around, before leaving.

+

At the police station, DS Cooper put down the phone. Having gone through the ledger of the hotel from today, coupled with the list of the people who were supposed to have been there twenty five years ago. Most of them had been easy to find, but one name stuck out from way back then a certain

Diane Saunders, she had booked for two weeks. But what had made DS Cooper interested, was the note in the margin, 'turned up without booking' written neatly alongside the booked time and date. He got up and walked over to look at the files, and in particular a telephone directory of this part of Sutherland. He opened it, then groaned, and put it back on the shelf. Next to it sat an old Yellow Pages dated from three years earlier. Now he took that and flicked through it to hotels. Cooper ran his finger down the list, and then took the book over to the photocopier and made a copy, he spent the next hour or so phoning the various hotels and B & B's in Brora, Dornoch and Helmsdale. After which, he had just to wait for the next day.

CHAPTER 31

DI Gray crossed the threshold of his office and stopped in amazement. DS Cooper stood there with some paperwork in his hand.

"You are in early, something come up?" He asked.

"Yes, there is one person missing from the list of people who were at the hotel twenty five years ago, and again this year. Well, not this year, but it's odd."

"Spit it out man." Said Gray as he sat down at his desk, pointing at the other chair as he did so.

"Diane Saunders"

"And she is?"

"She stayed at the hotel twenty-five years ago, but here is the thing, she, unlike all the other guests, didn't book ahead. Diane just turned up. Look there is a note in the ledger, see?" He swung the book around for Gray to look at and pointed at the remark written alongside the entry. "Now that got me thinking, I wondered if she was on holiday at the time. I have spoken to all the hotels and B & B's yesterday and asked them to see if they had records going back twenty five years. Ok, it's a bit of a long shot, but worth a try I thought. Anyway, there is one place that remembers her."

"Go on."

"The Riverside Inn, now called The Harbour Arms, they have a warren of cellar rooms. That's where the old records are kept from the year dot apparently. The new owners don't remember anything from that long ago, but they have a man who was working there then. They were going to speak to him when he next came in. Apparently, he is in most nights, nursing a pint all night, so they said."

"And did he turn up last night?"

"Yes, and he remembers the lady well, because she was often booking just a single night, about every two or three months. He thinks she use to bribe or blackmail people. He can recall taking on a man on one occasion. Just after the lady had had a discussion with this man, he, the man, suddenly needed to find money on a regular basis. Diane, is the name that he heard the lady call herself, don't ask how he remembered after all these years, but he said he would be happy for somebody to go and talk to him if we wanted to." Cooper stood looking at Gray hopefully. "Sir?"

"Very good, very good indeed. You had best go and interview him, and I'll look and see if she is on the electoral roll, or a taxpayer." He looked at Cooper, who had gone quiet. "What's the matter?"

"I've already done that, no Diane Saunders in East Sutherland, not at the present there isn't."

"You have been busy this morning haven't you?" Have you asked 'HOLMES' yet?"

"Not yet, shall I do that first?"

"No, you can go and interview this man, and I'll go down and input the name into HOLMES, see if it as good as they have always said."

Cooper left the office. Rising from his desk, Gray followed him out and went down to the computer room. He had taken the file from Cooper to get as much information as he could. The more that you could put into HOLMES, the better the chance of finding out something.

+

Diane had sat thinking back to how her life had panned out, a lot of things had happened since she had left Oxford all those years ago. It was a pity that her bag had been snatched on the last day of exams as well. Her little scheme that had been running in Oxford had netted her a nice amount. Enough to stayed in Oxford and settle down and keep the scheme rolling. Then she had been robbed, hadn't even noticed it had gone until she went to get something from her bag. Her boyfriend had suggested that she report it to the police, but she had said that wasn't going to happen. He didn't know of her scheme and she wondered what the police would have said if they knew that two thousand pounds in used notes were in the bag! She had been disappointed that things had gone so badly wrong but had put it behind her and moved Northwards. The boyfriend had stopped seeing her once she left Oxford. She wondered what had happened to him and to the person who had taken the money all those years ago.

Unknown to Diane, her boyfriend had seen inside the handbag. On the evening before when she had asked him to get her cigarettes and lighter from her bag. He had reported it to the police. As well as with a helpful description of bundles of money inside it. No, he didn't know how much. He had just gone to get her cigarettes and lighter. The police had been methodical in putting the details down and had promised to contact him or her if the bag and the money came to light. Nothing ever was heard of again. A bit like his relationship, once Diane had moved north.

+

HOLMES had done it's stuff and produced a list of 'Diane's and their associated last known addresses. A Diane Saunders was mentioned in a file from Oxford. A report of a stolen handbag, containing money, had been made by her boyfriend in the 1960's

DS Cooper had interviewed and noted what the man in Brora could remember from all those years ago, and now was at the office typing it all up. DI Gray stuck his head around the door.

"Got something, I think, or rather HOLMES has found a Diane Saunders."

"Where from?"

"Oxford, would you believe?"

"Oxford, Oxford, where have I seen that recently?" Cooper reached over his desk and pulled the list of names of guests out from under a pile of paperwork. ""Computers will make less paperwork they say", look at it." He pointed at the desk and floor overflowing with paperwork. "Ah, here it is. Well, well, a Mr Burgess has stayed there two times and he is from Oxford as well."

"Probably nothing to do with it."

"Bit of a coincidence though, don't you think Sir?" Asked Cooper.

"Perhaps. Let's go and ask him to see if he knew anything."

+

Jane and Bill had gone down to the Bar and after ordering their drinks had met with Thomas. They had all sat down together and found that they were telling each other what they thought or knew had happened.

"So, you were here twenty five years ago?" Asked Bill.

"Yes, and it is strange that we didn't meet up then. Do remember the death of the man who fell from the second floor?" He looked at Bill hopefully. Bill looked at him and Jane.

"Yes, that was a nasty accident, at least that was what the police said it was."

"Two deaths in a fortnight? An accident you say, I doubt it. Somebody knew something and was killed for it." Replied Thomas.

"Oh, come on, that may be the case in books, but this is real life, and people don't go around East Sutherland killing people." Jane said. The two men looked at Jane, then at one another.

"One was an accident, the other, the man just died, it happens you know.

It was just unfortunate that it happened in a fortnight." Said Jane.

"Oh, I know that, but stranger things can occur in real life, truth is stranger than fiction, or so I have been told."Thomas took a sip of his whisky and looked at Bill. "What's your line of work then?"

"Oh, just working out of an office based in London."

"Me too." Said Jane before being asked. "And you, what do you do?"

"Just retired, used to work in the Distilleries, Golspie and Brora mostly."

"So why do think the two deaths are connected in some way?"

"Well, the first may be real, as you say people do die. Falling from the second floor landing. The railings are more than waist high, so to accidently fall over one, well you would have to be very tall, or be 'helped' as it were."

"Have you told the police this theory?"

"Police, what use are they? I used to be regularly bl.." he stopped himself. "Anyhow I don't think they would be interested after all this time do you?" Thomas took another sip, then noticed that Ronald had entered the bar and was looking at him in a most strange manner. "Look it's been nice meeting you, but I have to go now."With that, he picked up his glass went over to join Ronald. Bill looked after him as went, then turned towards Jane.

"Do you think that he knows something? I always felt the second death was too easily explained away. The first one, well that was," he paused, "An accident, that was decided wasn't it?" He looked at her.

"I think that we should try and find out who the two men are that you saw, and sort that problem out first, don't you?" She smiled and then nodding at her glass, which was empty, "Another one please?"

He rose and went to the Bar and stood with his back to Thomas and Ronald in order to overhear what they might say.

"I think that we should send the second letter, it's been over a day, and she hasn't responded has she?"Asked Thomas.

"Not yet, but give her another day, then if she hasn't contacted us, I'll check at the Post Office tomorrow. We can then send the second demand for money. Time is on our side, we have paid the scheming.."

"Yes, yes, and I agree with you, she has had years of weekly amounts off me, and at least you had your capital returned." Said Thomas looking at Ronald as he did so.

"Yes, I know that, we discussed this at the Broch, now let's go about our normal business. We will meet again at the Broch tomorrow about three o'-clock?" Asked Ronald.

"Three o'clock, the second collection will have been collected. If she still hasn't got in touch, we can still catch the last collection." Said Thomas. They walked out of the Bar. Bill, having been served his drinks, made his way over to Jane. He sat down with the drinks and said quietly to Jane.

"You'll never guess what I have just heard, two of the men I saw are going back to the Broch at three o'clock, tomorrow afternoon. I can go and confront them. Get this sorted once and for all, as to what I saw all those years ago." He picked up his drink and looked at her.

"If it is the same men, then you really do need to tell the police first." Said Jane. "If it isn't them, you will look awfully silly." She smiled at him and took her drink off the table to take a sip.

CHAPTER 32

DI Gray stood inside the hall of the hotel, while a member of staff went in search of Mr Burges. Eva, the receptionist, had finished for the day, and nobody else seemed to know which rooms the guests were staying in. An older man came up to him.

"DI Gray?"

"Yes?"

"Sorry about the wait, Mr Burgess left the hotel a few days ago, and we don't know where he has gone to stay." He paused and produced a folded piece of paper. "But there is a list of the local hotels and B & B's that Eva was giving out to the guests that were having to leave. It was you who requested it, if I recall correctly didn't you?"

"Yes, I did say that, but, oh never mind. Give me that list please." Gray held out his hand and the man passed it over to him. "Don't suppose you know where Eva resides, I mean lives, do you?"

"Oh yes, that is easy. Eva lives in Golspie, in Lady Sutherland Road. Number forty one, if my memory serves me correctly." He smiled at Gray.

"Thank you sir, most helpful." Gray turned and went to the front door. Outside it was raining heavily, wishing that he had brought a coat he made a run towards the car. The door of the hotel closed behind him, and behind it, stood Ronald, looking at the man who had just given the list of places to Gray. The man appeared not to recognise him, so Ronald did up his jacket, before following DI Gray's example of running to the car.

Gray swung his car into Lady Sutherland Road. Wishing that it was compulsory to put house numbers on the gates or front doors of the houses. The hours he wasted looking for the right house, he thought to himself. Noticing that he was at the end of the road he braked and stopped the car. The number was on the front of that house, hurrah. He squinted through the car window, trying to make out the number, but it was no good, he would have to get out of the car and walk up the path to see it properly. The rain seemed to be increasing, but there was nothing for it, but to brave the elements. He got out of the car and slamming the door shut, ran across the road, and up the path to the number of the house he now could see it was forty. He looked across the road and to where his car was parked. The houses here were not numbered, so he had to go back a few, before Gray discovered the last one was 37. Now puzzled and soaked, he went back to the car and got in, the car quickly started to steam up inside, so he turned the engine on and did a quick turn of the car in the road and headed back to the Police station.

Once inside, he made his way to Cooper's office and walked in. Dripping water collecting on the floor as he stood looking at Cooper working quietly away, completely unaware of his boss behind him. Gray coughed loudly, making Cooper jump and turn towards him.

"Don't do that sir, you nearly gave me a heart attack. Can I do anything for you? You looked soaked."

"I am soaked, I am trying to find out where the hotel receptionist lives, I want to ask her something and she isn't at the hotel, and I was told that she lived in 41 Lady Sutherland Road. When I got there, it stops at 40 on one side and 37 on the other no 39 or 41. Explain that if you can. I am going for a warm cup of tea." He turned to go, and Cooper called over to him.

"That is easy, the property 37 bought the plot where 39 was supposed to go, but by then the council or post office had allotted the numbers to the houses. Though there is no 41, not to my knowledge anyway. I'll take a look at the electoral roll shall I Sir?"

Yes please, and you are looking for anybody with a surname of Fleming, there can't be that number living in Golspie." He turned and left Cooper to it. Twenty minutes later a bemused Cooper sat with strange look on his face. He had checked the electoral rolls and telephone directory. Not one Fleming in Golspie, Dornoch or Brora. had noticed though a Diane Bird with a property in Dornoch and in Golspie. He went to see Gray and found him in his office with a cup of tea sat on his desk. Gray looked up as he entered his office.

"No sign of Fleming but have found a Diane Bird, properties in both Dornoch and Golspie." Said Cooper.

"No sign of Fleming you say, but a Diane. Not called Saunders though is she?"

"No Sir, but how many Diane's' are there living in East Sutherland?"

"Not many, why don't you run a background check on her. Two properties you say? Must be rich to afford Dornoch and Golspie. Look in the morning I'll ask for some men to get out on the street.

We'll check the empty properties in Golspie, Brora and Dornoch. Then the B & B's and hotels. Fleming must be holed up somewhere nearby. You and I will go and try and find this Diane Bird of yours, unless you find out it is Diane Saunders under a new name.

+

That evening, Bill and Jane had visited the Police station and spent about an hour telling Cooper about what Bill had seen all those years ago. Cooper had listened and taken notes before they had been shown the main door. They ran across the car parked opposite the Police Station and got in as the rain hammered down on the roof of the car.

"Well, that was a waste of time." Said Bill angrily.

"Calm down Bill, what did you expect, after all this time, what thirty years plus? They have a skeleton in the attic to find out about, which is probably is their priority right now. Come on, let's go back to the hotel."

Ronald had driven to Dornoch, parked the car outside the Cathedral and made his way to the Jailers Rest. He stood in his room, having fished out the next envelope and added to the back of the envelope the new PO Box number he had purchased in Dornoch. Then weighing it in his hand, he looked across at the flat. No light showed he decided to hand deliver it. Outside the rain seemed to be getting heavier, so he quickly ran through the puddles of water and up the steps to the flat. He pushed it through the letter box and returned to the hotel. Diane, seated at the window, with no lights on watched with some fascination as he ran back to the hotel. So that's where you are staying is it, she thoughtfully said to herself. Then, still not turning on the lights, went and picked up his letter. Weighing it in her hand, she decided that she would go back to Golspie, she had only popped over to see if everything was ok, the streetlight had given her enough light to not need to put any indoor lights on. It was pure luck that she had been in the right place at the right time. Nobody would bother her here or in Golspie. She put the letter into her waterproof jacket pocket, buttoning it up fully, she pulled her hood over her head and left the flat to head towards Golspie.

+

The following morning, Bill had got over his annoyance at the Police not taking him seriously and they were both sat eating breakfast in their room, for a change. Jane reading *The Northern Times.*

:Anything interesting in that?" Asked Bill pointing with his toast to her paper.

"Not really, but it is local. Wonder where it is printed?" She turned to the back page and saw that it was in Golspie. "It is very local, printed here in Golspie."

"Really?"

"Yes, says it here." She passed it over to Bill and pointed to the bottom of the page. "Bill, they may have back copies, we could see if there is anything around the time when you saw the men fighting." Bill looked at her in amazement.

"Genius, that is what you are." He stood and went around the table and kissed her. "We'll go there after we have finished here."

+

An hour later, in the offices of *The Northern Times,* they had explained that they would like to see, if possible, some back issues from twenty five to thirty years ago. After explaining why, they were led into a small room with hundreds of red bound folders, in each one was six months' worth of back issues. Bill and Jane looked and saw they were dated, so started to look for the dates between 1954 and early 60's.

+

Fed up with Diane and her attitude, Thomas had decided to go and see her directly, he had phoned Ronald first thing. Ronald had found out that the Dornoch flat was empty. So now they both stood at the bottom of the stairs leading up to the flats in Golspie.

+

Diane who was now back in Golspie, sat up in bed refreshed after a good night's sleep. The sun had chased the heavy rain from the night before away. The air was fresh, and the smell of the sea came in through the flat's open windows. After getting up and having breakfast, she took another look at the lava lamp, still lying in its box, pity she hadn't got the second one, still one was better than two. She was sat at her desk when the front doorbell rang. Annoyed at being interrupted, she got up and made her way towards the door.

"Ok, Ok, I am coming." She said as walked down the corridor to the door. Opening the door, she was pushed back by Ronald into the flat, Thomas followed behind. Diane realised that she was in a very sticky situation. She led the two men into the flat. The look on both their faces, was enough for her to realise that this was not the time for being sarcastic. Ronald pushed her back into a chair and stood towering over her.

"So, didn't think we would find you?" Said Thomas, who now stood beside

Ronald looking down at Diane.

"Listen this is what we want you to do." Said Ronald.

"Both of us, get all the money we paid you and interest lost for those years and you leave the Highlands for good." Said Thomas.

"But I don't have that sort of money, not here anyhow. It would take me some time to get that together for you both. Anyhow, Ronald had his money back, as agreed, didn't you Ronald?" She looked at the two men, her eyes pleading, please believe me."

"Maybe I did, maybe I didn't. I get greedy, when I see you with these flats dotted here and there. Must have been doing the schemes
for years. What do you say Thomas?" Ronald nodded towards Thomas as he said that.

"Yes, years most likely." Thomas replied.

"What if I don't pay you?" Asked Diane.

"Oh, this is such a nice flat, all done out in these old items. They must be worth something. It would be such a pity to see any," Ronald went and picked a plate off the wall and dropped it on the floor, before grinding his feet in it. "damaged." Diane looked on in horror, the room was, as they said, full of valuable items she had bought over the years. Her eyes flitted to the picture on the wall of a horse. Thomas spotted her and went over to the painting.

"Valuable is it?" He asked as he took it off the wall.

"It's a Stubbs." She replied, nodding her head.

"I didn't ask what it was, I asked was it valuable or not?" He raised the large picture over the top of his head, as if ready to bring it down on to the floor with a crash.

"Don't do that." Diane cried out.

"Why not?" asked Ronald. His hand resting on the arm of Thomas, in a restraining manner.

"It's worth a lot, that's why."

"How much exactly?" Asked Thomas, as he slowly lowered the painting to the floor.

"Between eighteen and nineteen thousand pounds, maybe more." She replied.

"How much did you say?" Asked Thomas, as he looked at the painting in his hands. "Then I'll take this in lieu of any money." He grinned at Ronald as he said this.

"Don't be silly" said Ronald. You wouldn't get that amount if you tried to sell it, and she," he nodded at Diane, "would say it was stolen. Wouldn't you?" he asked her.

"No, but you are right, a dealer wouldn't give you anything like that amount, it's insured for that."

"How about that vase?" Ronald pointed to a china vase sitting on the shelf.

"A lot, about a thousand, give or take a bit." Diane said.

"So, basically, you are telling us you have no money, as it is all spent on these bits and pieces, is that right?" Asked Thomas. He had put the picture back on the wall and was adjusting it to make it straight.

"Yes." Diana sniffed, "Please don't damage anything else."

"Tell you what, we will give you a week to come up with the cash and that will give you time to sell some of these pictures and the like. What do you say to that?" Said Ronald with a nasty look at her.

"I'll try, but a week is not enough, I. would need to go to London to get the best prices."

"You aren't trying to get the best prices, you just need to get the cash we need, that might mean going to Inverness, but not any further." Said Thomas.

"But that means I will have to sell almost all of it." Diane gasped.

"So? We will be watching both flats, so don't think that you can get away to London or elsewhere. Don't even think of going to the Police. I know who killed two people at the hotel, don't I?" Said Ronald with a wink at Thomas. "Ok, we'll leave you for now. Now when you have enough money, or a week has gone by, put this lamp," He picked up the lava lamp , "in the window working. We will then know we can collect from you what is owed. Got it?" Ronald leaned in close to her face, as Diane tried to shrink back into the chair. She nodded furiously to him. "Good." Thomas grinned at Ronald and then they turned and left the flat.

Gray and Cooper happened to be walking towards the flats in Golspie as Ronald and Thomas came out and crossed the road to the car park. Gray looked across at the two men and thought he recognised one of them. However, before he could shout at them they got in a small car and drove off up Lady Sutherland Road.

"Sir?" Asked Cooper as they both stood outside the flats.

"Thought it was somebody I recognised. Yes, what is it Cooper?"

"A car is parked under the flats, so she must be in."

"Come on then, let's get it over with."

"What exactly do we want to find out?" Asked Cooper.

"Why didn't she book in advance of staying at the hotel. For that sort of quality hotel, you needed to be booking about three months in advance."They walked up the stairway and knocked on her door. Inside Diane was surprised to hear more knocking on her door. She picked up a brass poker from near the fireplace, and flung the door back wide. The two policemen stood there.

"Tell me Ms Bird, do you always greet people on the front door holding a brass poker, or is it just for our benefit?" Gray held up his warrant card. "DI Gray, and this is DS Cooper, can we come in please?" Diane nodded dumbly and put the poker down and walked back into the flat.

"Sit down gentlemen, can I get you a drink or anything?" She asked, hoping to delay the inevitable questions she thought they must be about to ask.

"No, we're fine thank you." Replied Gray. "We just need some clarification over a matter at the East Sutherland Hotel."

"Which is?"

"We were looking at the bookings over the last twenty five years or so, and it seemed that you didn't need to book ahead as other guests did back then, but just turned up. Now why didn't you book ahead, and how did you manage to get a room at such short notice?"

"But why are you looking at old records?"

"Just answer the questions please." Said Gray.

"Well, it was a long time ago, I can hardly remember things that long ago."

"That's ok, but we need you to try for us please." Said Cooper.

"If it is any help, two people died within the space of two weeks of each other at the hotel." Said Gray forcefully, playing the bad cop to Coopers good cop.

"Gosh, you're right, I should be able to remember that. Just a minute, I remember something about a man being found on the hall floor. Yes, that is it, I was in the bar at the time, and heard a scream, we all rushed out to see what it was, a man lay on the hall floor, I think they said it was just an accident? Anyway, there he was dead." Diane gave a little sniff.

"With respect, that was not what we asked you to tell us. How did you get in so easily, and what had you been doing before you visited the hotel?" Diane now realised that she was being questioned by two very experienced officers. So, deciding to tell as much as she could, she turned towards Cooper.

"I had been travelling down the East side of Sutherland and stopping at hotels where the fancy took me. They had a room, well a suite really, and I took it. Ask the receptionist, she probably has records and would remember me.

She was a bit snooty, if I recall. I didn't have much luggage, I try to travel as light as possible. I travel alone you see, nobody to help me in with the luggage, at most hotels that is."

"And where did you stay before then?" Asked Cooper.

"Brora or Helmsdale, one of the two. I can't quite recall which. There aren't that number of hotels in East Sutherland are there?" She smiled at Gray. "Anything else Inspector, as I do have rather a full morning. Some antiques to see.." She added, feeling foolish at once for doing so. Gray looked around the room, and his eyes fell on the horse painting.

"A Stubbs?"

"Very good Inspector, on loan as it were, I may be changing my mind about it, I don't think it suits this room, do you?" She rose as if to say I've finished and so have you. The two policemen rose and thanking her, left the flat.

Outside Gray and Cooper walked back to their car while Gray was deciding what the next move should be. Gray had a feeling that Diane was up to something, something bigger than they knew about. He would have to try HOLMES again, only adding Bird as another bit of information about Diane Saunders. He got out, and indicated that Cooper should go over to Dornoch, and wait to see if Diane went to that flat as well, and if so, if she came out with anything, or met with anybody they needed to know about. He would be updating HOLMES and seeing if anything else came to the surface.

+

Having shut the door, Diane stood by her window and looked down at the two policemen crossing the road to the carpark. First the wo men and now the Police with questions about things years ago. Things were getting a bit frantic. Looking at the picture, she decided that she would make a few phone calls. Going over to her desk, she opened a drawer before pulling out the notebook that she wanted. Thumbing through it, Diane found the number needed and went to the phone and dialled the Oxford number. A man's voice answered, quickly she asked if he still wanted a 'Stubbs' and if so, how much would he pay for one.

CHAPTER 33

Oxford 1990 August

A roasting 35.1C was hitting the sunny side of the streets. The ice cream sellers were doing a roaring trade., All the shops selling water had either run out or were close to doing so. Iced drinks had sold out by early morning, and now it was only midday. The man stood at the entrance of the shop and looked across to the gardens in the College, a gardener was busy on his knees weeding. A hosepipe snaked nearby, but nothing would be coming out of that for the fore-seeable future as hosepipe ban had been put in place. Gardeners were not happy. Watering Cans could still be used, but no hosepipes. He glanced at his watch, thirty minutes before the shop closed for a lunch hour. Their rule had always been to keep open throughout the day. Now though the heat had made most firms close to allow staff a bit of breather. Few staff would choose to go out into the heat. He had to though. A phone call had been received and there would be problems if he didn't make the visit to the antique shop on The High. Buses, full of hot tourists, kept flowing past the shop the loudspeakers saying the same message, "on your right you can see the world famous.." that was as much as he would hear, but he guessed, correctly, that the words Christ Church College would have been next. He turned back into the shop, the postcards on their stand seemed to be a tad old fashioned looking. That was only his thoughts, and he kept those to himself. He smiled as a pair of tourists came in asking for a map of Oxford.

Half an hour later, Justin left the shop and made his way up St Aldates to Carfax and along the busy High St. Forcing his way on and off the pavements, as the constant throng of tourists flocked towards him. He arrived at the row of small shops opposite the Examination Schools. Popping his head into the antiques shop, which was empty, nobody in their right mind would be buying antiques today, not even the mighty US Dollar was likely to be spent on this hot day. He rang the bell on the counter and a lady appeared from the back of the shop.

"Yes?" She eyed him up and down, as though gauging if he was a customer or a time waster.

"Is Ken in?"

"Ken?" She looked puzzled.

"Ken, he owns the shop."

"Oh, that Ken, sorry he has sold the business to me."

"When did he do that?"

"Last year, if it's any business of yours. Now what do you want? To buy or are you selling?"

"Selling, but on behalf of a friend. Would you be interested in a Stubbs painting?" She gasped, and then drew herself together.

"Young man, don't try and be funny, the Stubbs are all known in the Art World, and I don't think you have such a picture, but if you did, I would need to have it verified as a Stubbs, one can't be too careful, not these days. Would the person have provenance of the picture?"

"Not sure, but I can find out."

"Well, you do that, then come back. It would take about three months before any cash changed hands though."

"Ok, I'll be back." Justin left the shop. At once the heat hit him as though he had stepped into a furnace. Keeping in the shade he made his way quickly back up the High towards the Baskin Robins ice cream counter in Cornmarket. He had phoned ahead from his shop to order one of his favourites, mint choc and flake, double scoop.

+

In the Antique shop, she stood at the counter and thought to herself. A Stubbs, where could she fit it in to the shop. She looked around the room. It would be a draw right enough. She did not have much in the way of cash to even pay for it, but that could come later she thought to herself.

+

Dornoch in August was a pleasant enough place, not too hot, although the sun did come through the clouds now and then. DS Cooper sat in the police car, looking at the number of people who were making their way to the Dornoch Highland Gathering. The weather would make it pleasant, not too hot for the spectators and the participants he thought to himself. Cooper sat looking at the Cathedral. He was trying to remember when he had last gone inside any church building. Work always seemed to get in the way. Suddenly he noted that a car had drawn up outside the bank and Diane had got out, before it pulled away again. Puzzled by this, he knew she had a car, but obviously hadn't driven hers this time. He reached down and took a pair of binoculars from under the seat and swung them up and in the direction of the flat. Clear as anything now, he could see inside the front room, but only so far in. Nobody came into the room, then he saw a hand reach a vase on a shelf and take it down. Minutes later Diane appeared at the top of the stairs clutching a brown bag, it obviously was heavy, as she was using two hands to carry it down the stairs. Cooper, using the glasses he watched her walking past the Cathedral and across the green. Quickly Cooper got out of the car and throwing the binoculars onto the car seat before slamming the car door. He set off in pursuit. Diane, unaware that she was being followed, got to the shop, and walked in through the open door of the shop, and then straight out through the back. The owner had moved to the front door and had put the 'Closed for ten minutes' sign up. Was now closing the door as Cooper arrived, the owner shrugged her shoulders and pointed at the sign and closed and locked the door. Then went to join Diane out the back.

"What is that you have there? Be quick, I have customers waiting outside."

"My vase, I need to sell it, and quickly, look and tell me what you can give me for it?" She lifted the vase out of the bag and placed it on the table, the sunlight catching the blues and pale green swirls of the vase, and making it seem alive.

"I can give you six hundred for it, and no more. It will only fetch around eight hundred if I am lucky with an American tourist that is. You would get much more taking it down south."

"Don't doubt it, but I can't get away for work reasons for the next ten days or so. So, I'll take the money."

"Keep an eye on the shop, I'll go over to the bank and get some cash, I assume you want cash?"

"Yes, that would be great." The owner moved to the front of the shop, and took the notice down, before opening the door. Blast it, she thought, the customer has gone. She left the shop and headed across the square towards the bank. DS Cooper, now back in his car, had his binoculars trained on the shop. He watched as the owner came out and started to walk towards him. He wondered where Diane had got to, as she had clearly gone into the shop, clutching something and now the owner had left the shop. He quickly pulled out from the parking spot and drove and parked in the square. Cooper then ran quickly over to the shop and inside. Diane was seated at the back, reading a book, he turned to the right, once inside and started to look at some model cars in a display case. He was stunned at the prices on some of them. After about twenty minutes, during which a group of tourists came and haggled before buying a small but nice picture of the Cathedral, the owner came back. She hardly paid him a glance, but handed a bundle of notes to Diane, who then left the shop, as she passed him, she smiled.

"Learning about Antiques now are we DS Cooper?" She said as she left the shop. Damn! He thought to himself, she knew all the time he was there. He followed her out, but she had gone. The local bus had come in, and she was now sat on it watching him as he looked in desperation around the square for her.

CHAPTER 34

In Golspie DI Gray listened to Cooper as he explained how he had followed Diane and how she had seen him. She had not said anything, until she was leaving the shop. Where she had gone now, was anybody's guess.

"So, you have no idea what she sold to the shop?"

"None, well, it may have been a vase, but I can't be a hundred percent sure of that."

"Not to worry, I'll phone Dornoch, and ask them to see if anything unusual comes on display in the shop, and the price it is ticketed at. I wonder why she is selling stuff, strange that, don't you think Cooper?"

"Maybe she needs the money for something big."

"You may be right, at that Cooper. I think we need to take a look at the past files, anything concerning the hotel under either of the two names."

"Sir, did anything come on HOLMES about Diane?"

"Only the Oxford theft of some money and a handbag, and nothing else."

"And are they the same person? I tried to see if there was a connection, but couldn't find one."

"Don't ask me, not yet anyway. I suppose they could be." Gray looked at the ceiling and wondered what direction to go in next. "Come on Cooper, I'll buy you lunch." The two men left the office and headed out towards the centre of Golspie.

+

In *The Northern Times* archives Jane and Bill had found the mention of the two deaths at the hotel and the fire that had followed some years later. At reception they had asked and paid for, some photocopies of the relevant articles. Both were sat in the local park, reading and re-reading the documents before them.

"So, one death is accidental, then a person falls, from the second floor of the hotel, and then twenty five years later, a body is found in the hotel attic." Said Jane.

"That just about sums it up, and I don't think the first two deaths are connected, the first says the man died in the chair, another guest found him, but doesn't say which one." Bill looked across at Jane. "Good thing to, in my mind."

"Why say that?"

"I'd be dragged in for questioning and all kinds of things most likely. We are on holiday, or at least we should be."

"Bill, did the two men met again yesterday in Broch?"

"I don't know, it was pelting down with rain, remember?"

"I'd forgotten, as soon as this sun came out, that is."

"Did you look for the events of 1954 while you were in the records of *The Northern Times*?" Jane asked, looking at Bill slyly.

"Yes, a small note about somebody being admitted to hospital here in Golspie, a broken nose, and broken ribs."

They sat for a few minutes enjoying the peace and quiet, the locals were either on the beach or in the sea. Not much traffic flowed on the A9 through the town.

+

A Short way from them, Diane sat in her flat, overlooking Lady Sutherland Road, and the monument on the hill overlooking the small village. Her phone rang, and she picked it up at once.

"Yes?"

"Have you got the provenance for the picture? The buyer wants to be careful, says it will take around three months to verify and sell. I suggest you get some photos taken of it, and post those down to me, and any other stuff you need to prove it is what it is supposed to be."

"Yes of course, good idea. Keep in touch in the usual manner. Oh, and I'll send you something in the post, call it a sellers fee, once it sells that is." She replaced the receiver and got up and looked again at the picture on the wall. With a sigh, she took it down and over to the light, now where was her camera she wondered?

+

Dornoch Police had heard from Gray. A policeman, new to the area had been sent over to see if anything new was being added to the window. He had called in that a very nice blue and green vase, had been put in the centre of the window, and it was priced at one thousand pound with a plus VAT for UK residents label at its base. A group of visitors were busy looking in the window, having got off a coach a few minutes earlier.

+

At the East Sutherland Hotel, Eva Fleming had failed to turn up for work, normally known for being punctual. It had caused a bit of a stir. The manager talked of going to the police, but it was pointed out the police would not do anything for at least three days. After an hour of re-arranging staff, the hotel seemed to quieten down. Those guests still staying in the hotel, had had breakfast and now were either out in the grounds or back in their rooms. Thomas was in his room on the phone to Ronald, keeping him up to date with what was going on in Golspie.

+

The day before had seen Eva driving towards Golspie, planning to go home. She had noticed the fuel gauge was on the low side, so decided rather than turning and going to up to Brora, she would drive through to Dornoch where the petrol was marginally cheaper. Once the car had been refuelled, she had driven off back towards Golspie using the Embo road. When it had started raining heavily, she had skidded off the road, leaving both her car and her in a ditch. A road that nobody much used. She realised that either she could choose to walk to Golspie, some seven or six miles in the rain. Alternatively, she could stay in the car and hope that in the morning somebody would find her and help get her and the car out of the ditch. She also realised that her injuries could have been so much worse had she not been wearing her seat belt. The rain had continued all night making the ditch fill slowly all night with water. Now in the light of day, the car had slipped even more off road, and the driver's side now was high in the air, about three feet off the ground. With the door on the passenger side now in submerged water, and the other side high off the ground, Eva could not get out, even if she wanted to. It was around ten o'clock before a tractor, driving towards Dornoch, came to a halt in front of her. Since the road was blocked by the car, he couldn't get any further. He climbed down from the cab and walked over to the car, he tapped on the glass, as he could see somebody still sat there.

Stiff from a night in the car, Eva wound down the window and told the farmer what had happened. He returned an hour later with a pair of ropes and an attachment on the front of the tractor, lifted the car off out of the ditch and onto the road. She started the engine, it fired up, and then thanked him, before setting off for Golspie and her home.

Once at home she first called the hotel to explain what had happened, and then had a good long soak in a bath. Endeavouring to take some of the pain from her sitting awkwardly all night.

CHAPTER 35

Bill and Jane had decided to call in at the Police station and have another talk with the officer. Armed now with the relevant copies from *The Northern Times*, they thought the police may take a different approach to what had been going on in the past.

+

At the same time, Gray and Cooper had left Golspie, and driven towards the hotel. Gray was not happy about Eva not being around and her address being non-existent. They pulled up at the hotel and parked near to the door.

"We need to find out why Eva is not there anymore and who the previous receptionist was, and if they still have her contact details." Said Gray and they went up the stairs. Inside the hotel, the manager looked flustered as he tried to manage the reception area. A group of the remaining guests were tired of waiting and wanted to leave, despite Gray saying they couldn't.

"Ladies and Gentlemen, the police have said you aren't to leave the hotel, at least not to check out that is."

"But other guests have, so why can't we do the same?" shouted a voice from the back of the group.

Gray, entering the hall, overheard the last remark, and moved to the desk area.

"And you are Sir?" He asked the man who had spoken.

"David Gardner. How much longer are you planning on holding us here?"

"I'm investigating a murder, and it may be linked to some events twenty five years ago. All of you here, were here then as well. So, I want you all to have a really good think, did you see anything unusual then, or somebody you recognised then and again in the last few days. Once you have done that, and I'll give you an hour to do so, I'll come and talk to all of you, and then if I am satisfied, will take down your contact details and you can leave the hotel." A collective sigh went up, and mutterings of agreement rippled through the room, and the guests started to drift away one by one. Gray moved across the Manager, who was now looking a lot less flustered.

"You turned up at the right time Officer."

"Just a few questions, if that is alright with you Sir?"

"Of course, do come into the office." He led the way through and both officers followed him. "Do you want a drink?"

"No thanks, we'll just crack on if that is ok with you?"

"Perfectly." He seemed relaxed now he had got seated behind his desk.

"Eva, your receptionist. Do you know where she is?"

"Well yes, as it happens. She was involved in a small road accident, not hurt, but her car came off the road and she couldn't get any help till this morning, so we only just have heard from her. I've told her to go home and come in tomorrow. "

"Ah yes, her home." Gray took out his notebook and made a pretence of looking something up. "Forty one Lady Sutherland Road, Golspie. At least that what was I was told. Now I went there, and it doesn't exist. So, the question is, what is her real address?"

"Doesn't exist!" Exclaimed the manager. "Let me get her file out and I can soon tell you what it is." He reached down into a drawer and produced a file. After opening it and looking through it, he pulled a handwritten CV out, and passed it across the desk to DI Gray who looked at it and then passed it to Cooper.

"Thing is Sir, the address on this CV doesn't exist in Golspie. I wonder, if or when she turns up, you could let me know." He passed the manager the CV back along with a card with his contact details on. "You see Sir, there is a Lady Sutherland Road, a Sutherland Road, but there is no East Sutherland Avenue. Did you take up references from that CV?"

"Yes, but one said she was a good worker, the other one didn't reply. Really Inspector, I have a hotel to run, and needed staff, if I waited all the time for both references, the hotel would be empty."

"So, to sum up, you have a receptionist, who you have told to go home, and you don't know her address." Gray stood up and looked at Cooper, who did likewise. "Right, I am now going to spend as long as it takes talking to the remaining staff and guests." The two policemen left his office. The manager sat wondering what he had better do first.

"Sir, do you think.."

"Quite frankly Cooper, I don't know what to think, a missing person, a dead lady, who we have not managed to identify. Blast, I meant to ask him about the other receptionist." Gray turned to return ,and saw to his amazement, the manager leaving the hotel through the main entrance. "Cooper, you go and follow him. See if he goes to see Eva, and if he does, then we'll know where to find her." Cooper turned and followed the manager out to the car park, out and down to his own car. The Manager wasn't aware of him as he was intent on getting to his own car and driving off.

Inside the hotel, Gray walked back to reception and swung the book around to see who was staying in which room. Having made a note of that, he went up to the second floor. He glanced at the list, and walked around the shuttering, noting to himself that could be removed now. Knocking on the door of the Orkney Suite, where according to the list, a Mr Gardner was supposed to be staying. It gave no response, so he turned the handle, while calling out at the same time.

"Anybody home, it's the Police, we are coming in." Gray pushed the door open and edged into the room. It was empty, he made his way through the other two rooms, empty as well. Gray moved to the wardrobe, and opened the doors, nothing hung there. The en-suite showed no toiletries, but the towels were hanging in a rough fashion as though they had been used and put back. Gray was puzzled, nobody had left the hotel, well not as far as he knew, and yet the hotel room was empty. He left the room and made his way down a floor to the Suite marked Balblair on his list. This door was open but he knocked and called out as before. Then he heard the phone being put down, shortly after a man appeared at the doorway.

"Yes?"

"DI Gray, would like to have a word if that is ok, Mr Swift, isn't it?"

"Yes, that's right, Thomas Swift. Come in and sit down. What can I do for you officer?"

"I understand you have been in the hotel before, twenty-five years ago I think?"

"Probably about that, why?"

"We are re-opening the file on the death of the man who died then, it was deemed an accident at the time, but we are just checking to see if there is any other cause of his death? Can you recall talking to him or seeing him speak to anyone else at that time Sir?"

"Not really, I mean he was one of the staff, wasn't he?"

"Was he Sir? We are not too sure about that now. What made you think of that?"

"Somebody had said that I think, not really sure, not after all this time. You do understand?"

"Ok, that will be all. Can I have your home address in case we need to talk again please?" Thomas did that and Gray left the room, moving along to the Glenmorangie Suite to find Ian Reid already sat down and waiting for him. He stood up as Gray entered the room, and indicated for Gray to take a seat, which Gray did.

"I understand you want me to try and recall anything about the hotel and my visit twenty-five years ago is that right Inspector?"

"Couldn't have put it finer myself. You were here then I understand?"

"Just for a few days, had been a stressful year, lost my wife, cancer, and then with the job and everything else."

"Excuse me, what was your job back then?"

"Fireman, all my life. There was a fire here in this hotel, did you know that? It started in a room, just under the attic, and it could have been nasty, but for the quick actions of the receptionist, what was her name?" He paused to think.

"Eva?" Suggested Gray.

"Good grief no, she wasn't here then, it was, what was it, Sutherland, that is it, Flora Sutherland. Nice lady, nothing too much trouble if you know what I mean. I used to say, she had the wrong surname, should have been McDonald, with a name like Flora." He laughed.

Gray smiled wanly at him. "I expect she had that said a lot Sir. Anything else, what about the man who died."

"Which one?"

"The second one."

"Ah, that is a mystery. An accident or so you lot said at the time. I am not sure myself the height of the railings and two floors up. There had been no accidents in the hotel. Then within a short space of time, one man dies in the chair and then a staff member dies."

"Do you think it was an accident Sir?"

"No, I don't, I think he was pushed over the rails, everyone was in either the bar or the music room, easy enough to push somebody over the top, and nobody around to stop them." Gray noted this down, he looked at Ian, who was a small set man, and wondered if he could have pushed somebody over those railings. "You are wondering if it was me, well I couldn't have done it, I use to be at the top of ladders, lightweight you see, directing the hose at the fire. No, it wasn't me. Is there anything else Inspector, or can I leave the hotel now? I have put my contact details on here." He passed Gray a piece of hotel paper with the address and phone number on it.

"No, you can leave whenever you want to. You have been most helpful." Gray stood and left the room. Once outside, he walked along to the Old Poultney Suite, and knocked on the closed door. No answer came from within, so he knocked again, harder this time, but still no answer. Making a note in his notebook he went down the remaining stairs and out to the car park. Then he recalled that he had asked Cooper to follow the manager. Damn it, he thought. Turning, he started to walk through the grounds and down to the shore path and along to Golspie.

+

Cooper had followed the Manager out to his car. He had then got into his own car to follow at a discreet distance, the Manager to Brora. In Brora it turned right and drove down to the old fishing village and around to The Harbour Arms. He watched as the Manager went inside. Cooper drove slowly past. He saw the lights were mostly out downstairs except for a single light where a man sat at a desk writing something. Cooper parked under the bridge, wound down the car window and then taking out his binoculars he focused them on the door to the Inn.

An hour later, the Manager left the hotel and drove off. He passed Cooper, and didn't give him a glance. He turned left and headed Southwards. Cooper started the engine of his car and followed the manager southwards. He fully expected him to swing into the East Sutherland Hotel, but instead he drove right past it and on towards Golspie. Cooper, followed on at a safe distance. Both cars swept down the hill towards the castle, when suddenly the car in front vanished. Cooper, realising his mistake tried to slow down, but was going too fast and sailed by the entrance to the castle, on towards Golspie. As he got near the exit to the castle, he swung onto the gravel exit, and brought his car to an abrupt halt. Waiting to see if his hunch was right, the car shot out of the exit and straight onto the A9 into Golspie. Cooper drove after it, more slowly as they were now in the village. He noticed the car swing right up Lady Sutherland Road. Slowing down he turned right as well and noticed that it had once again disappeared. This time there would be a variety of ways it could have gone he thought to himself with bitter frustration. He slowly drive up to Back Road and pulling out slowly, looked both right and left, but no sign of any car. Frustrated, he banged the steering wheel and turned to go back to the office.

+

An hour later, found Cooper re- reading his report that he had just typed up. DI Gray entered the police station, tired and irritated, he knocked on

Cooper's office and sat down.

"Next time we take two cars. How did you get on, did you find where she lives, did he go there?" Gray sat back in the chair and sighed. He wasn't as fit as he had thought, and was tired from that walk.

"I did follow him, he went to Brora, The Harbour Arms, small place down.."

"Yes, yes, I know the place, cut to the chase."

"Well, he went in and was in there an hour, only the one light on. In the office I'd guess, and then he came out and drove to Golspie. He must have spotted me He turned off at the Castle, and then I caught up with him at the exit and followed him into the village. Then he turned up Lady Sutherland Road and disappeared. You know there are five ways he could go from there. Two to the left, two to the right and one straight up to the Mannie. Though I doubt he went up there. So, I drove to the end of the road and looked left and right. No sign of a car. So, came back here and wrote my report. I was just checking it when you came in. Did you learn anything new Sir?"

"Not really, just same old, did learn though that there had been a fire there. On the top floor under the attic it may explain why stuff was pushed to one side of the attic space. Spoke to a couple of guests, but here is a strange thing. One of the guests the room is totally empty, nothing in it. A Mr Gardner, register shows him as supposed to be still in the hotel, not checked out. Yet his room is empty, used mind you, but empty."

"Perhaps he moved rooms?"

"Perhaps, but unlikely, hotels don't usually like that sort of thing, causes more work, new sheets etc. You go back later and ask the Manager, if he appears again that is. Any idea as to the name of the skeleton in the attic? Sounds like a novel to me."

"No, but we did get a visit from two of the guests while we were out. They had been in before, and now returned with some copies of *The Northern Times* about the two deaths. I know you worked that case, but it seems to throw a bit of doubt as to the death of Mr Ross the man who fell from the second floor. I've been reading the articles, here." He passed the copies to Gray, who started to read them intently.

"This couple, they seem a bit more interested than the usual sort, wonder why?"

"The man saw some men fighting in the late fifties, up by the Broch, and it has always stayed with him, now he claims that one of the guests is one of the two men he saw way back then. I mean is that really likely?"

"Remember the hotel wouldn't have been built then though." Gray sat and thought about what he had just learned.

"We need to find those two and see if he can put a face to the man he thinks he saw it has to be one of the guests in the hotel."

Chapter 36

Oxford three days later.

Justin had received the packet containing an undeveloped film from Diane the day before and had taken it to a local photographic shop in St Aldates for developing and printing. Now in his lunch hour, he was hurrying up to collect it. He had asked for two sets of prints and was eager to see the results. He walked through the doorway and smiled at the young lady behind the counter, producing his order slip, she took it and looked under the counter at the assortment of returned items awaiting collection. She re-appeared clutching the red and yellow envelope, and passed it to him, having first looked on the front, to see that he had paid already.

"Here you are, hope you like the results." She smiled at him. Nice man, but she already had a boyfriend, pity, she thought to herself.

"Thanks." Justin turned and went outside and into the nearby pub to look at the photos. Ordering himself a drink, he made his way to the only free table and sat down before placing the photos in front of him on the table. Taking a strong gulp of beer, it was still hot outside, though it had dropped a bit in the last few days. He examined the photos, before putting three of the best ones together. He put the others, and the spare set, back into the envelope. The three photos, he put into the inside pocket of his jacket. He finished the drink and made his way outside and up and along to the antique shop in the High. He took a glance at his watch as he passed Carfax tower, he didn't have too long before he would be due back at work.

Justin speeded up walking and stepped out into the road. Keeping near to the kerb and almost running now, along the High, till he got to Queens Lane Antiques. He peered through the glass door, it was empty. He carefully opened the door to the shop, a bell jangled in the back somewhere. Justin stood getting his breath back, waiting for the owner to come through.

Ten minutes later, the three photos had been passed over and a promise of getting in touch had been made. Justin stepped outside and working out the quickest route back to work, setting off across and through Merton St and into Christchurch Meadow before cutting out through the Memorial gardens and back to work.

+

In Dornoch, Ronald stood in the phone box, and dialled the number for The East Sutherland Hotel. He asked to be put through to Thomas, he waited while the connection was made, then put in more money.

"Thomas, any news?"

"Not much, had the police here today, interviewing all the guests and staff. A DI Gray, clever so and so, be careful if you speak to him."

"What did you say to him?"

"Well, he wanted to talk about the death of that young man, the one who fell off the stair landing. Did I know him or seen him talking to anybody? I said I hadn't as I thought he was staff. Had to give him my home address though, and he wrote that down."

"What did you do that for?"

"He asked, caught me on the hop as it were. Cunning devil, you be careful. Any news on the Diane front?"

"A vase, priced at offers over a grand, has gone on sale in the shop window, a grand, I mean, who in Dornoch has that sort of money. I'll keep my eye on the shop, in case anything else comes through." The pips sounded, and Ronald hung up. Leaving the phone box, he walked across the square and took a look in the window. The vase was no longer on display. That didn't surprise him, an item with that sort of value could easily be stolen by smashing the main shop glass and reaching in and taking it. He walked on to his hotel.

+

Diane had spent the day choosing items to sell and phoning various shops and dealers in Inverness and further afield. She wondered if she would be able to part with the Stubbs. When she had bought it as a painting it had said on it. "After the school of Stubbs." The signature, though dark, looked to her like the real thing, and the price had been, in her eyes, steep, at eight thousand guineas. If it was a Stubbs, then her estimate to the two men of roughly eighteen to nineteen thousand would be way off the real value, trouble was, she didn't have the time to properly research and then sell. She wondered if she could slip off to London, take the picture, and have it properly valued at one of the larger auction houses. May be worth it, if they sold it for a lot more. May mean that the rest of the stuff in the flats would not have to be sold. She decided to go to the station and see what times the trains went to Inverness. Once there she could book a ticket on the Motor-Rail from Inverness to London, or if the times didn't suit, she could drive to Inverness and take the car, and the picture, down to London by Motorail. In fact, she thought to herself, that would be the better option. Deciding this, she quickly packed a few items. She stood and took the picture down off the wall. She carried it out and placed it in the boot of her car face downwards. Then after getting her overnight bag, she locked up the flat and went and drove off towards Inverness. Nobody had seen her leave Golspie, with a bit of luck, she could be back and nobody any the wiser she thought to herself as she drove southwards.

+

Eva, left her house and went out to her car before taking a critical look at the state of it. She decided to take it to Brora for a serious clean and fill up with petrol. She then would return to the hotel, the Manager was a good sort. He had dropped by last night and told her that the police had been to the hotel questioning guests and staff but would be gone by today. She knew she was taking a risk, her name wasn't even Eva, but sometimes names had a way of catching people out.

Eva, when she had first come to Golspie had found a small cottage at the South end of the village on the main road. Fortunately for her it had a back entrance off a side street. The front was old and decaying, and she kept it that way, less likely that people would knock or be nosey. She just went in and out the back and left the front room as it had been when she rented it first. The back and upstairs were now completely different and had been made into a nice area, the money had run out. The person developing it had gone bust and her landlord, seeing an opportunity, bought it for a song at auction and started to rent it out. The price of the rent was low, but she could afford it and wait for her chance to do what she really had come to Golspie to do.

Chapter 37

Now back at the hotel, Bill and Jane sat looking at one another in the bar, both had empty glasses in front of them, and were nursing a second glass of drink. Bill looked around the hotel bar, musing what it had been like twenty-five years ago. Jane caught his eye and smiled at him.

"Penny for them?" She asked.

"Just recalling what it was like when we first arrived here."

"It was different, that I'll grant you. Do you feel happier, now the police seem to be taking a bit more interest?"

"Yes, though it would be nice to know who that man was. The few guests that are here and we have seen them all, doesn't look like any of the two men at all. You'd think he would be here in the hotel The police said for everyone who was here then to stay put."

"Maybe he was a criminal on the run." Smiling as she said so.

"You might be right, I know you are joking, but think about this, he steals a wallet. Returns back here when the hotel is built and two people die. Now a third body is found, the receptionist has gone missing. It is all a bit too much of a coincidence for me." He drained his glass and nodded at Jane. "Another one?" She shook her head. They both rose and left the bar, and taking her arm in his hand, he led her out to the main hall, and on out to the gardens.

+

Dornoch had been busy with tourists. The vase, displayed as it was, in the shop window, had quickly sold. The tourists had bought a lot of the items from the hotel as well.

Diane had been to London and had her picture valued. The consensus at the auctioneers, was it was in the school of Stubbs, rather than by him. Value around four to five thousand pounds at best. Did she want to leave it to be sold at their next auction they had asked. She had said no to that. Now she was driving to Oxford, to speak to the person who she had spoken to, if her hunch was correct, she would easily sell it in Oxford. Her plan, then was once sold, to catch the motorail from Oxford to Glasgow and drive on up from there to Dornoch. First though the antique shop in Oxford beckoned. Diane had phoned ahead and found out that parking outside was very much forbidden. She decided to park in St Clements car park, the closest she could legally park to the shop without attracting the attention of the police. Something she was keen to avoid. She parked at the only space she could find, right at the far end of the car park. Then taking the picture out of the boot of her car, she started to walk to the shop…

…Twenty minutes later she was inside showing the picture to the owner, who was most impressed. Unlike the auction house, she was convinced that it was a Stubbs, and was prepared to pay a reasonable amount, half in cash, half by cheque. Diane, happy with the agreed price, said she would accept that. The owner closed the shop to go to her safe and take the cash out to give to Diane. Diane left the shop, feeling for the first time, she had got back control of the situation she had found herself in. Smiling as she walked down towards Magdalene Bridge, she was roughly pushed off the pavement by two men, dressed in smart suits.

"Hey, watch where you are going, I could have been knocked over." She said, as she got back onto the pavement. One of the two men, grabbed her by her wrist, and marched her down the road and turned into Longwall St. "What's going on?" She demanded as he swung her against a phone box.

"Now you listen and listen good. We got a word that you were back in Oxford. Our boss, he has a long memory, back in the sixties, you owed him for some 'stuff'" He rubbed his thumb and finger together, "You had credit, you had always paid before, he gave you the good stuff. Trouble was, he never got paid though did he? Two thousand pounds, that was a lot of money then, still is, but the thing is, the value has gone down, so he wants some interest on top of the two thousand, as well. You get my drift?" He twisted her hand behind her back, and she screamed with pain. The other man, stood looking the other way, making sure nobody was going to come to her rescue. A couple of tourists looked on but ignored her and walked on past.

"Yes! Stop twisting my arm. I can explain."

"Oh, you can explain, well how about you explain to the man himself, he is getting older now, but his memory hasn't faded. Not yet anyhow." He swung her around and a black Jaguar pulled up alongside, the door was opened, and she was pushed into the car, the door slammed and drove off. Diane sat upright, she was not alone in the car, sat beside her was an old man, well he looked old, but was probably in his late fifties, she thought.

"Hello Ms Saunders, or should I say Bird? I've been looking to have a chat with you since the sixties, naughty girl, not paying for the stuff, gave me a bad name, I had to get out of Oxford, get my drift?"

"Yes," She struggled to put on her seat belt, daft she thought, when he could probably arrange to have her killed any way he chose. "But listen, I did intend to pay you. I had the money ready in my handbag, but I got robbed. I don't know who took the handbag, but they had the money as well. I can give you the money in few days, how about that for old times' sake?" She looked at him hopefully.

"Oh, for old times sake? Do you have Thirty Six grand then?"

"How much?" Screamed Diane.

"Quiet, I am being reasonable, you see, the two thousand has had inflation and interest added to it, that is what makes the total of Thirty Six thousand five hundred and sixty pounds, but I'm asking for just the Thirty six grand, call it a cash discount for old times sake?" He smiled cruelly at her. I assume you do have that sort of money, having just sold the Stubbs?"

"Not as much as that, she had to make some money from the sale, I have some here, and the rest is a cheque, look here it is, if you don't believe me." Diane fumbled in her bag, and produced the cash and the cheque, trembling, she handed it to him.

"Not bad, for a picture, that is not a Stubbs is it." He said, looking at her with a glare. "This will do for a start, but you need to get the rest to me by tonight."

"Tonight, how am I supposed to find that sort of money in an afternoon?" She spluttered to him.

"I don't really care, sell one of your houses?" She gasped, as she realised he must know a lot more about her than she had first thought.

"How much do you know?" She asked.

"Everything, I know about the property in Dornoch, and Golspie. Sell the flat in Dornoch, that should get the rest of the money."

"But I couldn't sell it that quickly, it takes time to sell these days. Give me some time. Please." She realised though, that he wasn't the sort to give her more time. She watched as they drove out through North Oxford and towards the ring road and the Golf Course. How long was it since she had originally left Oxford, she wondered to herself? A fool, she should have gone straight to him as soon as she was robbed but had instead run away to Scotland. She saw him smile at her, and then car turned into the Golf Club. He looked at Diane, and she wondered what would happen next.

"I've always fancied a property in Scotland, give me the flat, and I'll say we are quits. I had my solicitor here to draw up the English side of the legality, presume you have a Scottish one?" She nodded. "Good, then we can progress as arranged, you get to keep the flats in Golspie, and I get a nice Dornoch flat and all the contents. Agreed?"

"Agreed." Said Diane, realizing that she had run out of options.

"Good, so glad that we have sorted out the past, we can put it behind us now, and move on. Get to know each other better, as we will be neighbours, so to speak."The door opened, and she unbelted her seat belt and got out, one of the two men who had grabbed her, stood there, clutching a briefcase. The boss, got out of the car on the other side, and walked round to Diane, he handed her handbag, less the cash now.

"I'll let you keep the cheque, you need it to pay off your other problem. Oh, by the way, I think I know who took your money all those years ago, do you want to know who?"

"Yes, if you really know that is." She hissed at him.

"He worked in the University, a man called," He paused and put his finger to his mouth as if trying to remember. "Ah yes, Burgess. Don't know where he is these days, he was living in Headington, but hasn't been there now for some time.

"Burgess! Diane exclaimed.

"Yes, do you know him?You need to get your money back from him, along with the interest of course. I've told you how much that is, so just go and ask him for the same amount, and if he hasn't got it, I am sure he has other assets, if you get my drift?"

"How do I get back to Oxford from here?" She asked.

"Take a bus, they run every twenty minutes or, so I am told. Now just sign the documents, here, here, and here." He pointed to a paper on a clipboard that one of his men had passed to him while they had been talking. She took the board and signed away her flat and its contents, not having any other choice. She looked up as she did so and wondered what sort of connections he had to know her movements. He could see the way she looked at him, what she was thinking, and said to her. "I have contacts all over the UK, and a few in the main London Auction Houses.There aren't that number of Stubbs that are not known about. When a lady makes an appointment to show an auction house her 'Stubbs' then I put two and two together, along with the name, and send a bit of money and a whisper or two around my network, and voilà! I get what was mine, and interest back. I won't say it has been a pleasure, as it has taken me years to find out about you and where you live. Goodbye." He turned and left her standing in the car park, as he and the other two men walked towards the Club house. She turned and walked out towards the main road and the nearest bus stop.

CHAPTER 38

Eva sat at her desk, listening to the man on the phone, he had phoned her about an hour ago and had asked her to phone him back within the half hour she had now done so and was on the phone listening, rather than speaking, as he told her what was going on.

"In essence, I have the money back and a flat as well, I think that will be enough, I didn't expect her to come down to Oxford, let alone London. I think you had better come South, but before you do, I want you to go to her Solicitors, and get a key once the paperwork has come through, no cash involved, so it shouldn't take too long. I just want to make sure that the contents are still there, I doubt she will try and empty the flat. Though she might try and take one or two choice bits and pieces with her. Go and stay in Dornoch, there are a few places to choose from."

"But what about my job at the hotel?"

"Best you leave it for now, I understand the police are looking into the deaths of two people up there, and you don't want to get too close to them, especially with no legal paperwork, do you?" She heard him laugh, but to her it was no laughing matter, she had come to the UK on a student visa, and had overstayed her time. Now being on the wrong side of the law, she had been easy prey for the likes of him to offer her a good job, and a false reference. She did some real work, got one real reference, and then moved from job to job with his reference as one of the two needed. She could find out the security of the properties, and if two or three months later, after she had left, the place got robbed, well that was hardly her fault was it? He hung up, as she replaced the phone. She looked around her and with a sigh, went to the roof and took down her two cases, and started to pack. Having to move just as she was starting to like both her job and her place where she lived. The phone rang, jolting her out of her thoughts, and she answered it, her hand slightly trembling.

"Yes?"

"Ah Eva, glad I caught you, when do you think you will be back at the hotel, today or tomorrow?" She looked at the calendar hanging with the photo of the castle on the month displayed. She didn't need to leave today, did she?

"I'll be up this afternoon, I need to talk to you anyhow."

"Fine, I'll see you about two?"

"Two o'clock." She hung up and carried on packing her few bits and pieces together.

Ronald had driven over to Golspie to meet Thomas, he had not seen or heard of any movement since the vase had been sold. He wondered if Diane was stringing them both along. Parking in the carpark overlooking the sea and after walking along the sea front, had cut through beside the flats and not seen her car. Fuming, as he knew she wasn't in Dornoch and by the look of things nor in Golspie. Ronald walked quickly back to the car and drove out onto the road, nearly crashing into a lorry that was driving North. Accelerating out of harm's way, he soon arrived at the hotel and parked before he ran up the steps and into the hotel. Ronald looked down the hall, nobody about. Running up the stairway to the first floor and he knocked loudly on Thomas's door. A few minutes later, the door opened, and Ronald pushed his way roughly into the room.

"Have you seen any sign of her? She is not in Dornoch."

"Probably at the flat then." Replied Thomas.

"I've just come past there, no car."

"Maybe she has sold it to pay us? Did you try the doorbell?"

"No. But there were no lights on, and the lava lamp is not in the window, lit or otherwise." Said Ronald

"Do you think she has run off?"

"Maybe, but I can't see her leaving the flats, and her items can you?"

"Can you break in to the Dornoch one, check it out?" Said Thomas.

"Now don't be silly, we don't want to draw the police into this do we? Best we wait two more days, the week will be nearly up by then. She may have gone to Inverness, we said she could go that far, didn't we?" Replied Ronald.

"You might be right. Ok, you go to Dornoch, and ring me if you see her or her car." Thomas said. Ronald thought for a few minutes and then nodded agreement. He turned and left Thomas's room, and walked down the stairwell, to the hall. At the same moment, Bill and Jane were leaving their room. Just along from Thomas's and Bill saw Ronald as he went down the stairs. Bill turned to Jane.

"That's the man I saw, let's go after him." Suiting the action to the word, Bill turned and ran after Ronald down the stairwell, but Ronald had too much of a head start and by the time Bill got to the door of the hotel, Ronald was already starting to drive off, Bill remembering the number plate, returned to the reception desk and grabbing a bit of paper and a pen, quickly wrote down the number. Jane walked up to him.

"You didn't catch him then?"

"No, but I do have this." He produced the number on the piece of paper. "His number plate, the police will want this, then they can talk to him." Jane sighed.

"Bill, they aren't going to do that, for a thirty year old,"

"No not that. The fact is, I can remember seeing him here, when we were here before"

"So?"

"So, if all the people who were here twenty-five years ago have been asked to stay, and he isn't staying here, why isn't he? I bet there is a good reason for him not being here."

"You don't know that Bill, it is just supposition on your part."

"Look, if he had a room here, he wouldn't have gone out in such a tearing hurry would he?" Bill looked at Jane, with a pleading look.

"Ok, why don't we go and tell the police, let them handle it?" Jane suggested, after a moment's thought. Bill nodded and, after checking he had his car keys, they walked out towards their car.

+

Twenty minutes later, Gray sat beside Cooper as they listened to Bill and Jane telling them what they had seen. Then passed the car number to Gray. Gray had taken a quick look, before passing it to Cooper.

"Run that through the ANPR system for me." Cooper rose and left the other three looking at one another. A few minutes later, he returned and passed a printout to Gray. Gray read it, and smiled, then turned to Bill. "The car number is registered to a hotel, not seven miles from here. The Harbour Arms." This might be a first link in a chain, we'll take it from here, but if you find out anything else, then contact us as soon as possible." Gray stood, indicating the meeting was over, Bill and Jane rose, and Gray stuck out his hand. "Thank you for this information, we can start to do things now, that we couldn't before." They both left him and went out onto the street where their car was parked in the small layby in front of the police station. As they did so, Jane noticed Eva leave the house next door, and walk across the road to the car park. Jane nudged Bill.

"That's our receptionist. I wonder where she's been? The Manager said he didn't know where she had got to."

"That's none of our business, come on, let's go for a drive." Bill started the engine and they drove north out of the village and on to Brora. As they passed the hotel, Jane touched Bill's arm.

"We could always try the food at The Harbour Arms. It's almost lunchtime."

"Yes alright, but doubt that DI Gray will be very pleased." As they approached Brora, Bill swung the car into the layby and turned to the back seat. He picked up the map lying there. Having found on the map, The Harbour Arms, he carried on driving. Five minutes later, they pulled up outside and looked at the closed up building, with a hand painted notice on one of the boards. "For SALe " and a phone number underneath it. The e had been squeezed in, as though the room that the capitals had taken was too much. Bill reached out and touched it with the back of his knuckle. The paint came off on his hand. Jane had got out and had taken a photo of the outside. Then turned and taken a couple more of the harbour. Down in the harbour, along with several small fishing boats, was a nice modern sea-going boat, with internal engines. In the silence, the sound of its engine ticking over could be heard between the screeches of the seagulls. Jane tapped Bill and he turned to her.

"See the boat, now that looks so out of place, and this place," She indicated with her thumb, just closed, any connection do you think?" As she spoke, she took a close up of the back of the boat, 'BAR HOUR' I'll just take another one," but Bill grabbed her, propelling her back into the car,. He had seen what she hadn't, two men, were now walking fast towards them. He started the engine and did a sweeping turn, so that he now faced them, and put his foot down, raced towards them.

"Duck!" He shouted, pushing the car faster, through the small winding streets. Jane did as he asked, just as a shot rang out and the back window cracked. Bill, swung the car round a close bend and up the hill, keeping down low and slowed slightly once he couldn't see any other car following them. He reached the end of the street and turned left onto the A9. Jane looked at him before turning and looking at the rear, now broken, windscreen.

"Bill, what just happened then?"

"I think we turned up at the wrong time, I'll go and tell Gray this, he'll want to see for himself." Bill relaxed as he drove on towards Golspie.

+

If he had, but known it, Gray and Cooper were busy driving through Brora, the opposite way that Bill had just left, and had parked opposite The Harbour

Arms. They had got out and walked across to the Inn. Like Bill, Cooper had touched the newly painted sign and had discovered it was still wet. Now bending down near the harbour, he was brushing his hands through the grass, in an attempt to get the paint off. His left hand knocked off a rusty ring set into the ground. He looked at it, attached to it was a mooring rope. Cooper followed it with his eyes and noticed it dropped over the edge of the harbour. He stood and walked down to the edge, and pulled it up, it was cut. He turned and called out to Gray.

"Sir, over here a minute." Gray half ran and half stumbled down the grass verge, and up to Cooper.

"What is it?"

"Cut mooring rope, think we just missed something going out of the harbour."

"Blast, it's got away. It will obviously be a large boat when you see the size of this rope, compared to the ones used by the small fishing boats." Said Gray.

"And somebody who has a very sharp knife as well." They walked back to the car, as they did so, Gray caught sight of something glinting on the road in the sunlight.

"Just a minute, something is in the road." He walked over and bent down and picked up a cartridge case. "Now who would be using a shotgun around here?" He reached into his pocket and producing an evidence bag, carefully picked up the cartridge and put it into the bag, before sealing it. He walked back to the car and told Cooper to drive back to Golspie.

CHAPTER 39

Eva walked into the hotel, her bags were packed in the hall of the flat, this wouldn't take long she thought to herself. She caught sight of the Manager walking towards her.

"Good to see you, are you recovered from the accident?" He said as he guided her into a nearby room that had been set aside for the disabled bedroom. He indicated for her to sit down, and he sat opposite her. "So, I want to have a chat with you, one or two things are starting to get me worried." She looked anxiously at him, had he found out about her real purpose for being there, she wondered?

"Just a couple of questions, and then you can go."

"Which are?" She sat more upright.

"What do you know about the death of Sarah Peters?" He leaned back.

"Who?" Eva asked. She had never even heard of the name, let alone meet her.

"Sarah Peters. The police asked me to look out some details of guests that had stayed here twenty-five years ago and more recently. Fortunately, the paperwork had been stored in the basement, and although a bit damp, still readable. While I was looking back twenty-five years, I found the paperwork for a Miss Sarah Peters, like you an overseas student, and then she disappeared. A bit like you did, before we knew about the car accident that is. So, I ask myself, why it is such a similar event, occurring in the space of twenty-five years. When I look up the paperwork for you and her, the reference for one of the two references I ask for," he paused and looked at her hard. "is the same name and address. Now Sarah Peters, she was a housekeeper, like you were. Then Flora retired, and you got promoted. Now the thing about housekeepers are they have access to the whole hotel. They know all the spots where stuff may get hidden until later. Now I ask myself this, given the fact that Sarah disappeared about then and still remains what is the connection, if there is one. Low and behold, I find that items have been taken out of the hotel, and got rid of." Eva looked at him.

"Do you mean the stuff from the attic? That part that had been bricked up, and nobody knew about? That stuff?" She said with as much emphasis as possible, "That stuff you told me to deal with?"

"Yes, when I said deal with, did I ask you to get rid of it?"

"Well, no, but that was what I thought you meant."

"Look this can be sorted out quickly, just tell me who you sold it to, and we can go and get it back, or if it has sold, the cash for it. " He paused. "Unless you have already got the cash with you? How much did you get for it? Only, I saw a nice lamp in Dornoch recently and it was priced at a thousand pounds. Now I am not saying that was in the hotel, but it might have been, or similar items, items that you thought, nobody has seen for years, hell, they probably doesn't even know about them, what harm can it do? You are right, it doesn't do any harm to the hotel. It does do you some harm though, you lose you your job and your trustworthiness going forward. Now if I can have your sets of keys please?" He held out his hand, and Eva looked at him and then reluctantly fished in her handbag and handed them over to him. "Thank you, is that all the sets you have, none stored back at the house, wherever it is you really live, that is."

"What about my pay, and holiday time?" Eva was panicking now, as she realised that without cash, she couldn't get far, certainly the man on the phone wouldn't give her any.

"Ok, here is your last pay packet, made up to today, and includes your holiday time that we owe you." He held it towards her and she made to take it, but he took it back out of her reach. "Now, you get this, once you have taken me to the shop or business where the stuff was got rid of. I assume you do have details for that, do you?"

Eva nodded silently cursing the day she had phoned the shop. "Good, then we can go now can we?" She nodded again, looking at the envelope that he held. Wondering how much was in it and how long that would last, and would it get her to Oxford? He rose and signalled that the meeting was over. Eva followed him out of the hotel and down to the car park. "We'll take my car, I'll be coming back and you can get a lift." She got into the car beside him, for a few mad seconds wondered if she could grab the steering wheel and push him out, but dismissed the thought as soon as it had come. He started the engine and drove off down the drive gathering speed as he did so.

+

Cooper was driving along the road towards Golspie. Bits and pieces were starting to come together, but still needed a few more bits of the jigsaw. He was running over events in his head when a car just shot out of the hotel right in front of him. Desperately Cooper pressed the brake pedal to the floor willing the police car to stop, but there was no way to avoid it, the police car slammed into the side of the car and spun across the road, the airbags inflating and deflating just as quickly. Very shaken, Cooper got out of the car, as did Gray who had been sat in the back lacking the airbag, he had crashed into the back of Coopers seat and was now nursing a cut head and a bleeding nose. Once Cooper saw Gray was out of the car, he raced over to the other vehicle, and looked inside, two people a female and male were bent over, and were not making a sound. Cooper reached into the driver's side, through the broken window, and turned off the engine and took the keys out. Then he gently shook the driver, but nothing, he felt for a pulse, but there wasn't one. He moved around the car to the other occupant, who was now making sounds of somebody about to be sick. He opened the door and helped her out and led her to the side of the road. Traffic was now starting to pile up on each side of the accident as completely blocked the road. Gray had sat down, with his head bent over, on the verge of the road and was trying to stop his nose bleed. Cooper looked around him, satisfied that there was no risk of fire, he looked up the drive to the hotel, and started to walk towards the entrance, this was not going to look too good, he thought to himself as he arrived at the door to the hotel. Once inside, he looked around for the receptionist, nobody there, and then deciding that time was of the essence, turned the phone on the desk towards him and dialled 999 to report the accident and ask for all three services to attend.

At the Golspie Police Station, Bill and Jane had just started to give their update, when all hell broke loose, policemen started to run out of the building, leaving the pair of them behind, as police cars set off with wailing sirens, to join the noise of the ambulances and fire engines.

"What the?" Asked Bill, but Jane shrugged her shoulders.

"Big accident by the sound of all three services. I doubt we will be a priority somehow, let's leave a written version and get back to the hotel, they left us some paper and pens." She pulled a pad of lined paper towards her and started to write..

+

Ronald had pulled off the main road at the top of the Mound, and had turned towards Lairg, with the roads now smaller, it would be easier to see if he was being followed. He stopped at Rogart and went into the small shop and bought a paper and some food. Once outside again, he noticed that his was the only car in the car-park. Pulling out onto the road, he carried on driving towards Lairg, which by a roundabout route would eventually get him to Dornoch.

+

Thomas, along with all the guests, heard the noise of the three sirens and had gone out to look. Realising that it was at the bottom of the drive and the traffic was not going to be going anywhere in a hurry. Some chose to go and look, while others returned to the warmth of the hotel. He had remained in the hotel. He wondered where the receptionist was and why the desk was un-manned. One of the other guests had told him that a policeman had been killed and that was why the number of cars with flashing lights were on the scene. Thomas had smiled but thought it much more likely that they were trying to clear the only road going North to Wick and Thurso but didn't say as much. At the scene of the accident, the first ambulance had taken Gray to the local hospital and another had taken the passenger to the hospital for her to get checked over. Policemen had accompanied both as until Cooper talked to somebody higher up, nobody had any idea of what had happened.

+

In Oxford the man tried again to phone Eva but got nothing but dialling tone. He hung up and turned to his Boss.

"She isn't answering the phone."

"Well keep trying, she has to come back sometime. Something is going on up there and I need to know what. Until she gets the keys to the flat, I don't have a base to work from."

"I could go up and take a look for you?"

"You? Give me a break. I'd go myself, if I had somewhere to stay."

"What about her place in Golspie? You know the guy who rented it to her."

"You might have a thought, get him on the phone, I need to speak to him now. Once you have done that, keep trying her number." He turned and took a cigar from the humidifier and cut the end off, before lighting it and after a few puffs, gave a contented sigh of delight.

CHAPTER 40

Eva woke up in a hospital bed. She looked around her, a headache was starting to come on, and she took a few minutes to realise where she was and why she was in a hospital. A Policeman sat on a chair beside her bed, he was reading a paper. A bell was on the table beside her, so she reached out and pressed it. A few minutes later, a nurse appeared and took her temperature. Looking at the reading, she smiled at Eva.

How are you feeling Miss Fleming? That was a nasty crash you had, good job you were wearing a seatbelt and the car had airbags. Do you want a mirror?" Eva nodded, she was wondering how she looked. The nurse passed a mirror and Eva saw. The cuts and bruises that covered her arms and face, though fortunately for her, the bruises were starting to fade. She looked at the nurse.

"What day is it?"

"Saturday, you have been unconscious since the accident."

"How long ago was that?"

"Two days. The other man is dead." Eva looked stunned, as things started to come back to her. The Manager firing her and then driving her to the shop, but they hadn't got there. The car had been hit by another car and then this. The good news, she supposed, was that the shop didn't need to know anything else. The bad was that she hadn't got back to Oxford or collected the blasted key to the flat in Dornoch. Shivering, Eva realised that he, would not be placated, by her story of the accident. He had asked her, no told her, to pack up and go South. Why had she gone back to the hotel she asked herself. Her thoughts were interrupted by the Policeman giving a small cough to bring her to his attention.

"If you can just tell me what you can recall happening and if you know who the other man was as we have yet to identify him Miss." He sat there waiting for her response.

"He is, was, the manager of the hotel. We were going to get some," Eva paused for a minute, "..supplies. We pulled out of the drive, and another car, " She shuddered as she recalled it, "Hit us on the driver's side, I think it was braking, but can't be sure. That's all really. Sorry." She looked across at him as the nurse left the two of them.

"That's fine, we'll get this typed up, and you can sign it, though don't leave the area, my boss may need to speak to you." He folded his notebook and looked over towards her.

"Oh, that is not possible, I have to go to Dornoch and then to Oxford." Why had she told him that she wondered to herself?

"Well, I don't suppose that will matter much, as long as you don't leave the country."

"Do you mean Scotland?"

"No, the UK."

"Ok, I'll let you know when I get to Oxford where I am staying, shall I?"

"That is perfect. Now you get some rest, you have had a nasty shock." He turned away from the bed and left the room. Once the room was empty, Eva got out of the bed, and slowly made her way over to a cupboard, that she hoped, held her clothes. Opening the door, she saw that it did, and quickly got dressed. Just as Eva had finished dressing, the nurse returned with a Doctor in tow.

"What are you doing up?" The Doctor asked her.

"I need to get to Dornoch, and I don't feel too bad." She replied.

"Ok, let me just check you over, and if I think you are fit enough, and you are young and healthy, you can leave, if not, then you stay put. Agreed?"

"Yes." She replied as he checked her eyes, and pulse, then smiled and nodded to the nurse.

"She can be discharged." Eva smiled at them both and stood up.

"Can I leave now then?"

"Yes, but do take it slowly at first. Did you say Dornoch?"

"Yes, I need to get there, but first I have to go back to my home to collect some stuff."

"I'll drive you there." Said the nurse. "I am just ending my shift."

"Oh, you don't need to bother yourself, I can easily walk,"

"Nonsense, it's not any bother. Just wait there, and I'll come and get you." The nurse turned and left her alone in the room.

+

The Nurse had dropped Eva off, outside her small house on main street, it hadn't taken her more than a couple of minutes to collect her two cases, and now she had walked to the railway station. A notice had said that next train was due in about half an hour, so she decided to sit and wait. She had decided not to go to Dornoch, instead to try and get away from the man in Oxford, though she realised that might be difficult with no references to speak of. Still that bridge would be crossed when she came to it.

+

The boss looked over to his henchman and snarled. For two days he knew that his man had been trying to get hold of Eva, but without success. He also had learnt that Diane had left Oxford and had last been seen heading towards London. He had found out where the Stubbs had been sold, and had the shop watched, to see if anybody would buy it. Currently the shop had a photo of the painting on display inside the window, with a notice saying, 'Enquire within'. Apparently a lot of people had looked, but nobody, yet, had actually gone into the shop. Still it was early days, he thought to himself. Bending towards his desk, he picked up a letter opener, made in the shape of a deer's head, and sharpened to a point, and started opening the post that had arrived that morning.

+

Ronald was fed up with being in Dornoch, there hadn't been any sort of activity at the flat, and of Diane, there hadn't been a sign of either. He had kept a close eye on the flat, but it remained in darkness and locked up. Thomas had kept him up to date with what was going on in Golspie. That was a lot, apparently a police car had hit another car, and the driver had been killed, the passenger was injured but survived. He ran his eyes down the classified ads of the local paper, nothing about flats or items of antiques. Folding the paper, he tucked it into the inside pocket of his jacket and went out for a walk around the town. When Ronald got level with the flat, he noticed that Diane had parked her car outside the bank, indeed, he could see the front door was wide open. Deciding that this was as good a moment as any, he quickly ran up the few steps and into the flat. Diane had her back to him, and with the door open, hadn't heard him enter. She was busy packing some small antiques into two cases, wrapping them in tissue paper first, and then placing them amongst lots of other tissue in the cases. Ronald watched fascinated, as Diane moved around the room, selecting some pieces, and rejecting others, it was obvious she was choosing the best antiques for herself. He silently withdrew and made his way to a phone box to call Thomas and update him on what he had seen.

+

An hour later, Diane had finished, and turned to take the two, now full, suitcases, down to her car, but blocking her way were Ronald and Thomas.

"Going somewhere without paying us? That is naughty." They indicated that they all should return to the flat. They all went back inside, and Thomas indicated with his hand that she should sit down.

"This ours?" Thomas asked her.

"Yes, no, you don't understand." She replied.

"Then tell us, so we do, I thought it was easy enough, sell a few items, pay us and you get to live in peace, or Dornoch." Said Thomas.

"So, what's changed?" Asked Ronald with a queer look on his face.

"Oxford, that's what has changed."

"Oxford? It never changes, it's fixed in the past, the dreaming students and their dreaming spires." Sighed Ronald.

"I don't have the money, and will never have it, understand?"

"Oh, come on, you have this, and the flats in Golspie." Thomas waved his hand around the flat.

"I did, but I owed a man some money, a lot of money, and now he wants it back with interest." Diane paused and looked at Ronald. "You ever been in Oxford?"

"Why, what's that got to do with anything? Yes, I live there, now can we get on."

"Certainly, did you live there in 1960?"

"What is this, twenty questions?" Asked Thomas. Ronald was now looking a bit red around the colour.

"May have done, why?"

"You see, I don't think I owe you anything, rather the other way around. In 1960 I was a student and going to repay the man I owed the money to, after my exams. I had taken the money with me, and on the way across the street, I was robbed, robbed of a lot of money, but you would know that, wouldn't you Ronald?"

"Me? Why would I know that?"

"You were the man who robbed me, at least that was what I was told in Oxford."

"If you knew that, why didn't you report it?"

"I didn't want the police knowing about my money."

"Dirty money was it?" Asked Thomas with a sneer.

"No, just some stuff that I sold to other students, to help them concentrate. So, Ronald, can I have my money back now, it would be around Thirty Seven thousand pounds, but I'll not be greedy, I'll settle for thirty six thousand." She watched him as he sat down and looked at her. Thomas stood looking at the pair of them.

"I don't know what game you two are playing, but I want my share of the money I paid you Diane, so if I can have that, I'll leave the two of you to sort things out for yourselves."Thomas said.

"A cheque be alright?" Diane asked, as she rose and made her way to the partner desk in the window.

"For cash?" Asked Thomas.

"If you want." Diane wrote the cheque and passed it over to Thomas, who looked at it, and then at both of them again.

"Right, I have my share, sorry Ronald, but you two seem to have some history, and I don't want to be a part of that. See you around."Thomas left the room and they heard him going down the stairs. Diane turned to Thomas.

"It was you, wasn't it?You took the money and." She paused. "and I want it back, I have lost this flat and all the contents because you stole my handbag all those years ago. Now it's your turn to pay."

"But I don't have that sort of money. Not in the bank anyhow."

"Neither did I, but I didn't have a choice, I had to sell. I have come to choose those bits and pieces that I like. Not that are the ones that are worth a lot, he would quickly realise that, if I took the good stuff. Mean to say, that there is some good stuff in here, but not enough for him to notice. So, do you have a house?"

"Yes, in Oxford."Ronald looked at her, and realising that it was quiet probable that she might have been the student that started him off all those years ago, besides why she would lie to him?"

"Then you can sell it and give me my share."

"I could do that." Said Ronald, as he thought of the house not being his, and wondering where in the world he would find to live out his days.

"But?There is a but coming, isn't there?" Diane snarled at him. "There always is a 'but'."

"But, would that be the end of things, I know how your little schemes work, a bit of money now, and each month going on and on."

"Not this time, just a cheque, and you don't see me again. As I see it, I hold all the cards right now.Your turn." She stood and looked down at Ronald. He looked up at her. He realized that she did hold all the cards and he had nowhere left to go. He had nearly that amount in a savings account and wondered if she would take less, worth asking he thought to himself. He looked up at her.

"I can get some of that now, well at the bank, and the rest later."

"How much are we talking about?"

"If the bank contacts my bank, and it goes smoothly, twenty five thousand now, and the rest later." He looked at her and she laughed, then bent down close towards him.

"Listen up Ronald. You owe me a lot of money, and I know that you killed at least two people and probably can pin the third one on you as well. Remember I saw you kill the old man in the music room. What was that man called?" She paused, and Ronald broke in without thinking.

"Bertie Parker."

"Poor Bertie Parker, whatever had he done to hurt you. Maybe he saw something he shouldn't have, was that it?" Diane asked.

"Maybe."

"So, this is what we are going to do, go down to the bank, you get the money transferred, and I take the cash, and a bank draft for you, which I will bank in two months' time, time enough to sell your house and send me my proceeds. What do you think?" But Ronald had got up and leapt towards her, grabbing her around the throat. Diane struggled to take his hands away, but he was too strong, she felt herself feeling faint, and a darkness was coming over her, she collapsed onto the floor. Ronald still carried on choking her, then finally she was still and he removed his hands. He now looked at Diane and realized just what he had just done.

Now he stood and shaking, he made his way towards the decanter but stopped just in time, as he realized that his fingerprints would have been on it. He quietly made his way to the front door and closed it. Then he stood still inside the flat, still shaking, and looked around the room, what had he touched, apart from her neck, he didn't think he had touched anything else. He made his way to the kitchen, and saw a bottle of bleach on the side, a cloth was on the draining board, he picked up the two together, poured some onto the cloth, and then went and wiped her neck where his hands had been, then keeping the cloth and bleach, he wiped the front door handle both inside and out and left the flat. He pulled the door closed, using the cloth and then walked down the steps and on the way to the hotel, dropped the bleach and cloth in a couple of litterbins. With a bit of luck, he thought, they would be emptied and on the rubbish tip by this time tomorrow. Once at the hotel, he checked out and drove to Golspie. He needed to sort out some things with one or two people before heading south to Oxford he thought.

CHAPTER 41

DI Gray had recovered enough to be back at work and was catching up on paperwork. The woman in the crash had gone to Oxford, she had telephoned from Inverness saying so. The written report from Bill and Jane was being read very slowly. He realised that the Harbour Inn had something to do with this but was not sure what. The boat that Bill and Jane had seen had been identified as belonging to the Inn and with a name like BAR HOUR, should have been as easy as anything to find. Despite calls to the Coastguard and the river patrols, no sign of the boat had been seen. Indeed, if it hadn't been for the photos that Jane had taken, he would have had difficulty in believing it existed himself. He stood up and was about to leave his office, when there was a knock and Cooper stuck his head around it.

"Sorry to interrupt, a nurse at reception, says she wonders if she might have a word or two, it's about a lady called Eva, Eva Fleming, she said." He looked at Gray hopefully.

"Show her into interview room two, I'll come along." A few minutes later, the nurse, Cooper and Gray were all seated in the interview room.

"I wonder if you know where she might be, Officer. The lady discharged herself, well the Doctor did really, but she wouldn't have stayed. Anyhow, I dropped her off at her house and then I did expect to see her in the village. Since then I haven't seen a sign of her. So, I came to ask if you knew anything? I mean she was involved in that car crash."

"Excuse me, did you say you dropped her at her home. Where exactly was that? You see the address we have, doesn't exist."

"Oh no Officer, this exists, I watched her go in, in my car mirror." She smiled at the two officers.

"Well can you show us where it is, if we drive you down the street?"

"You don't need a car, it's next door to you. The small detached house."

"Wait a minute, the house adjoining the station? Next door?"

"Yes." She watched as the two men got up together, and left the room, then Cooper stuck his head back around the door.

"Thanks, you can go now, that was very helpful." With that she was left on her own. She stood up, shrugged her shoulders, and left the police station. Looking up the street, she could see that the front door of the house was open, and she assumed they had got in somehow.

Next door Gray and Cooper were looking through the house, it was evident that nothing of a personal nature had been left in the property. There was a piece of paper by the phone, with a few numbers scribbled roughly on it. The handwriting was not great though and both men had struggled to make sense of it. Cooper had put it in an evidence bag and carried on looking through the property. Gray was in the living area and stood at the door looking at the dust that lay everywhere, he slowly closed the door to the room and went to the kitchen, which by contrast to the previous room was clean and modern. He was taking in the fancy new cupboards, having opened one or two, and found nothing in any of them. He turned as he heard footsteps coming through the hall and into the kitchen, a tall dark haired man stood in the doorway, he took one look at Gray and turned and left.

"Hey, you there, stop, police." But the man had left the house and by the time Gray got to the door, he had vanished. Gray looked up and down the street, but now no sign of the man. With sigh, Gray turned and went back in to carry on searching the kitchen.

It was Cooper, who had found it, tucked in the bedroom under the bed, a lava lamp, with a dent in the base, and a small sticker saying 'The Grand East Sutherland Hotel' on the base. He had plugged it in, and it had worked. Cooper had, when he brought it out, felt something on the base, and on closer examination, had found it looked awfully like dried blood. It was now in a large evidence bag and stood on the kitchen counter with both men looking at it.

"Do you think it might be a murder weapon?" said Cooper.

"Who knows. We need to get it tested, and see if it is blood, it looks as though it came from the hotel, with the sticker on it and all."

"Bit dusty I thought." Said Cooper.

"No more than it should be if it is as old as I think. Look, you get this down to Inverness. Get them to check it over, and ask about the blood, is it blood, or something else, and its age, approximate or real, on you go." Gray indicated towards the door and watched as Cooper left him alone in the property. Sighing, he bent down and took another look under the counter of the kitchen, the kickboard ran along the length of the units, but near to the washing machine he noticed it didn't go inwards and along the side of the washing machine. Curious now, he pulled lightly at the open end, and with a bit of effort, pulled it away from the legs of the kitchen base units. Wishing he had brought a torch, he squinted down the length of the units, and thought he saw a packet at the back near to the wall of the kitchen. He carefully replaced the kickboard before leaving the building and closing the door behind him, made his way to the police station next door.

+

Inside, a man was telling the counter officer, that his house, next door had been broken into and what were they, the police, going to do about it? If they moved quickly they could catch the two men responsible. He was told to fill in a report and leave it to them. Sniffing loudly, he did as he was asked before then walking out of the front door as Gray was walking in the side entrance.

+

The phone rang in the luxury apartment in Gloucester Green, a man lifted the receiver and then after listening, went, with the phone, to find the Boss. He wasn't going to be very pleased, he thought to himself.

"Yes?"

"Boss, listen, the Golspie house, it's been broken into, two men broke in. I've reported it to the police, but they don't seem interested, even though they are next door to it. The two robbers were in the house when I went to check up on Eva. What do you think we should do?"

"We do? It's not my problem. Wait a minute, did you say that you went to check on Eva?"

"Yes, haven't seen any sign of her around the village, has she left her job at the hotel, only I have not heard anything from her, about the best bits to go, you get my drift?"

"Yes, I do, and I am getting to like it less and less. She is supposed to be getting the keys to a flat, I have been given, in Dornoch. I told her to get the keys from the Solicitors, just a minute." He walked over to the desk and opened the drawer and looked at the name written at the top of the paper. "Here you are, WS. Robin and Batman, no not Batman, Bannerman." They are based in Dornoch, or so it says here on this piece of paper. Go there, I'll phone them, and get the keys to a flat in Dornoch, it's above the bank. Ring me back when you have got in the flat. She may be hiding in there."

"If she was Boss, then I wouldn't be able to get the keys would I?"

"Right, but if the Solicitors say they haven't got the keys, then I'll know she is playing some sort of game with me, and I don't like games do I?"

"No Boss." He hung up and went over the road to collect his van, before driving to Dornoch. 'The Boss' was not a man you said no to, he had witnessed that too many times. Mind you, he had to admire how the old man ran things from as far away as Oxford. Even down to the Inn being 'emptied' of the problem. He smiled as he thought of the quickness of that boat getting away from Brora harbour, probably the biggest thing the harbour had seen in its life.

+

Bill and Jane sat in the TV room of the hotel. Bill felt that something was missing from the puzzle, he realised that the person he had followed was the same person who he had seen as a boy, and that telling the police up here was the right thing to do. Then there were the bigger problems to solve, and the skeleton in the attic had been just another one to add to the growing list he had. They could both hear workmen clearing the rubble out of the room on the top floor, decorating and refurbishment could be allowed to proceed, at least that was what the hotel had been told, it seemed to be in a ghost style, with no receptionist, and no manager, the rest of the staff were trying their best, but things were being left, like clearing away dirty crockery. Jane sat reading a local history of Brora, and occasionally looked over towards Bill.

"Do you think we will ever know what went on in Brora?" She asked.

"Not sure, it looks as though it is part of the bigger picture, somebody who has the means to be able to afford to close an Inn at short notice as well as organizing a fast, sea-going boat. That is not something that you would expect to find in a small fishing port, well would you?"

"No, and I am sure that the local Police may have something we don't or can't get to know about." She looked over her book at Bill.

"You're right as usual, now which do we look into first, the body in the attic or the man who I saw attacking and robbing the other man?"

"Might they be linked?"

"Don't know, the police haven't said how old the skeleton was, not yet anyhow."

The Management of the hotel, or to be precise, the Owners and Directors, had finally got around to realising that the hotel, despite the staffs best efforts, would not run itself. One of the Directors had driven up from Luton to take charge and employ some staff. She was now looking at the paperwork piled on the desk of the manager, and sorting through it, into piles, one for rubbish, one for filing and one for action. The action pile was growing taller by the minute, and was in danger of toppling over, but she ploughed onwards. An hour later, finished, the pile for filing were now in two box files, the rubbish had been shredded, and the action pile was being sub-divided into today, and put off to tomorrow, piles. The bell rang in reception, and she ignored it to start with, then remembered there was no receptionist to deal with it. Sighing, she rose and went through, two policemen stood there at the counter.

"Good afternoon, DI Gray and DS Cooper. We are in the process of looking at three deaths connected to this building, the most recent, well the longest being the recently discovered skeleton in the attic. We think we have identified who it might be. Can you please check and see if you or your predecessors ever employed a Sarah Peters?" Gray looked at her with a smile on his face. She looked up and smiling said.

"You are in luck DI Gray, I was just sorting the paperwork, and for some reason, her file is here on my desk." She offered the file towards him. Gray opened it and scanned the pages, reading the addresses to Cooper for him to note down. He handed it back to her.

"Thank you, that was most helpful, by the way you can use the attic again now, thanks again." They both turned and left her to her sorting.

"Bit of luck finding that file Sir, wasn't it?"

"Luck, maybe, but ask yourself this, why was it out at all, a file from that long ago, out on the desk of the manager."

CHAPTER 42

Inverness had confirmed that it was blood on the base of the lava lamp but had no way of saying it belonged to the skeleton that was found in the attic of the hotel.

Gray had put the forensic team on checking the house next door. He had also found the report of two men breaking into the house and had realised that was probably him and Cooper. He had spoken to the owner and smoothed things out over a glass at The Doe Inn. Forensic had found the packet under the kitchen cabinet, a fine quality uncut stash of pure cocaine. He had been told it had a street value of one hundred and thirty one pounds, on the streets of London he thought ruefully to himself, not the streets of Golspie.

The team had also deciphered the scrap of paper, with two numbers on it, one in Brora, that had been found to be The Harbour Inn, the other number was an Oxford one, but the engineers at BT were not being that quick in finding out whose exactly. Gray had chased them a couple of times but had been told that with over one hundred and twenty thousand population, and a lot had two or more numbers, it wasn't going to be a quick job finding out whose it was.

Cooper had managed to find out that The Harbour Inn had been shut for about ten years, then new owners had bought it, done some work to just one of the bars before re-opening it. Locals had stayed clear, after being warned off, it appeared to be a front for some kind of business, though what had yet to be found out. Gray sat back in his chair, and sighed. There were too many threads to try and decipher all of them, and as Cooper had said, to him that morning, they might not be connected.

That couple from the Hotel Bill and Jane, he thought they might have found out something else, but they hadn't. He re-read the paperwork that they had left and wondered why a small village like Brora would have had gun wielding criminals around, shooting at cars. The cartridge had been identified as being made outside of the UK.

Of the boat, the 'Bar Hour', well that had been a red herring if there ever was one, the photo of the rear of the boat, on close inspection, had shown it was simply a board hanging on a couple of hooks. Easily to change the name he thought. It was a pity that they, Bill and Jane, hadn't been able to identify the type. He had put requests at the other local stations in Dornoch, Helmsdale, Brora and Wick to see if the boat appeared in any of those places, all having harbours it could have put into, but it had vanished into the blue.

+

Eva had managed to get to London, a large enough place to hide, she thought to herself. She knew that 'The Boss' had contacts across the UK, but London was a big place, and if she found some honest work, perhaps not what she had done in the past, but something new. Then maybe there was a remote possibility that she would not be found by him or his gang of crooks.

+

Ronald had been to the small antique shop, no sign of anybody and it was closed as well. He had packed and left Dornoch, but not before saying a few farewells to the few folk he had meet, he didn't want to leave in a hurry and for that to be remembered as unusual by anybody. The flat hadn't been touched, although he knew that state of affairs would soon be changed once the body was discovered.

+

After talking to his contact in Golspie, The Boss, having arranged a few things in Oxford, had finally arrived in Dornoch. The journey had been long and arduous he thought to himself, as he pulled up outside the Cathedral and turned the engine off. He made his way to the nearby bank. He had passed one on the way in, but that didn't have a flat over it, he noted the stairs going up the side of this bank, presumably leading to the flat, well he could check that out later tonight, when there were not so many people around. Meanwhile, he decided to get some cash from the ATM and have a meal nearby. He knew he would need to find somewhere to stay, as the house in Golspie still had the Police crawling all over it. His contact had told him they had found the kilo of cocaine in the property and were now like a dog with a bone, convinced that there was more somewhere nearby. The police had dug up the back garden, nice of them he thought with a smile, as that would have been the last place he would have hidden anything remotely like drugs.

+

An hour later, after a nice meal in a nearby restaurant, he decided to not stay in Dornoch or Golspie, come to that, but drive to Brora. A nice hotel overlooking the Golf Course, that would be perfect and the last place the police would look for me, he thought to himself.

+

His car pulled up outside the hotel, a small golf course was nearby, and it overlooked both the harbour and 'The Harbour Arms' so he could keep an eye on the place. He asked for and got a room overlooking the Harbour and it's fishing boats tied up for now. Later, he would go and have a look at his property both here and in Dornoch. He had signed the register under the name of 'Patrick O'Conner.' Didn't want to use his name, it was too well known across the police forces of the UK, though in Scotland that might be different.

+

That evening, Bill and Jane had driven back up to the Le Mirage again, for another fine meal. The had stopped off at Brora harbour at Bill's suggestion, and now had parked just a stone's throw from The Harbour Inn. Not close enough to be seen, but to watch if anybody walked nearby or showed an interest. Sure, enough around eight thirty a very short man driving a sports car, pulled up outside the Inn and after looking up and down the street, proceeded to go to the side door and unlock it before going inside.

"Bill, we need to tell the local police, not Gray, by the time we have driven to and from Golspie and explained, he could be gone."

"I agree. We passed the Police station on the way north, it's just on the outskirts of the village." So, saying, he started the engine and was about to drive off, when he looked at Jane. "You drive and tell them, I'll stay here, see how long he stays inside or if he leaves, then I can at least say when and what direction."

"Ok, but don't do anything silly now will you?"

"Have I ever done that?"

"Plenty of times."

"Ok, but mostly due to work." He got out and Jane walked around the back of the car and got into the driver's seat. Bill had vanished into the night. Jane sighed and drove off towards the Brora Police Station.

+

Inside The Harbour Arms, Patrick had been looking out through a net curtain on the first floor, he had seen the car driver get out and change over with the other passenger, but not seen the first driver get back in. Bending down he carefully retraced his steps and found what he was looking for. A set of high quality binoculars. He made his way back to the window, parting the curtains and put the glasses through the gap before looking and focusing them on the dark side of the street opposite. Satisfied now, he could just make out the shadow of a person standing against the wall of the old ice store. Well, he would have a long cold wait. Patrick put the glasses down on the floor by the window, and left the room, carefully closing the door after him. The old servants staircase, hidden behind a wall, was the way he had made his way up to the room and he went back the same way, making sure to close the doors after him. Walking into the Bar, he noted the mess that the police had left, but there didn't appear to be any empty glasses indicating they had been free with the drinks. In fact, that was very odd, as far as he knew, it had been vacated very quickly indeed. Going behind the bar, he lifted the trapdoor and went down into the dark cellar. He groped for a light switch and finding it, switched it on, nothing happened. Patrick made his way back up the stairs to the bar, he had thought that the electric was off, but the lights under the various pump signs were all lit. Cursing quietly, he decided he would come back next day, in daylight, that would be riskier, but he would get a torch at the local shop and be better prepared.

+

Outside Bill had not seen any sign of the man, but had noticed the side door was now opening, albeit slowly, a hand had appeared and then the man had come out of the building and turned and locked up again. For a while, he seemed to be looking straight at Bill, but Bill thought it very unlikely that he could be seen. He had already noted the car's registration number, and now watched as the man got back in and did a three point turn, before driving off past Bill, out under the railway bridge and onto the A9, where Bill saw him turn left. Minutes later, Jane drove back up.

"Get in, the police want to speak to you. Gray is on the phone waiting to talk."

"You must have just passed him."

"What the sports car?"

"Yes."

"So, what do you want me to do?"

"Follow that car, he drove out and turned towards Golspie."

"Bill, if we talk to Gray, from here and he will be able to stop it, as it will have to drive through Golspie."

"Good thinking." She swung the car around and drove off in the same direction as Patrick had done,

+

Eva had found a small job in a bookshop, an independent one, on Charing Cross Road. Five doors along from one of the biggest bookshops in England. She had been half truthful in saying that she wanted a change of career and her last manager had died in a road accident. Hence the inability to give him a reference. She had told them the name of the hotel so they could check the accident out, if they wanted to, she thought to herself. A small B & B on a side street had been happy to take her money, money that should have been going to Oxford to pay 'The Boss' as he liked to be known. She had felt that a new beginning meant that he would be unlikely to find her easily. Halfway down to London, she had remembered the cocaine, hidden in the kitchen, she doubted that the Police would find it, and if they did, well it wasn't as if it had her name and address on it was it? She smiled at a customer came into the shop and made her way forward to greet them.

+

The lady in Oxford Antiques shop looked up as the doorbell rang. The Stubbs had not sold, a lot of interest, but no real takers, she wondered about putting it into a London auction, one of the bigger houses she mused. The man seemed to be taking a goodly interest in the picture she thought as he approached the counter.

"Is that real?" Asked Ronald.

"Yes, I paid a lot for it. Are you interested at all in it, Mr?"

"Burgess, Ronald Burgess. Is it newly on the market then?"

"Yes, discovered in London, or that was what I was told."

"London eh? You would think it would have been better selling there than in Oxford wouldn't you?"

"Possibly, now are you interested or not?" She snapped at him. Really, she thought, timewasters, PTW she called them to her assistant, if such a person came in. (Professional Time Waster).

"I am very interested, can you hold it for me, here is a cheque for a deposit, I see you are asking thirty six thousand pounds." He bent and wrote a cheque for seven thousand two hundred pounds and passed it to her. I've not made it out to anybody, but think that a twenty percent deposit is fair don't you?"

"Very fair, I'll not bank it, but will take the picture off sale and put it out the back for safety."

"Very wise, I'll be back in two days." Said Ronald as he left the shop.

CHAPTER 43

Patrick had made his way to Dornoch, driving along the back roads, he had just missed the roadblock on the A9, something he didn't realise. Now in Dornoch, he had got into the flat by gently forcing the catch on the front door. As he opened the door, the smell hit him first, then the flies which swarmed out of the flat. He pushed the door with his foot, and it swung back without a sound. Cautious now, he walked in to the flat, careful not to touch anything and saw the body of Diane lying on the floor. Being careful not to disturb anything, he gazed around the flat, and saw the two cases in the hall, tempted though he was to take them, he realised that if he removed them, chances were high that there would be two spaces in the dust showing where something had been standing. No, he thought, better to leave things as they are. He could claim the flat later, after all the fuss would have died down. Retracing his steps, he carefully closed the front door, using a handkerchief to pull it closed before going back to his car. He sat in the car, thinking things through, he had now realized that he couldn't have the flat, too many questions, he wasn't even sure the paperwork would stand a deep scrutiny by the Police or a firm of Solicitors, better to cut his losses here, and concentrate on Brora. He turned the car and then drove out and across towards Brora. At the mound, he pulled into the layby, and phoned the police, he just left a short message, that he was reporting a burglary in a flat above a bank in Dornoch. Hanging up, before too many questions could be asked, he drove on towards Brora. He drove again along the back road of Golspie missing again the roadblock that Gray had set up to trap him. Within forty minutes of entering the flat in Dornoch, he had sat down in the reception area of the hotel in Brora, in front of a roaring fire and was reading *The Northern Times*.

+

DS Cooper was at the roadblock, he looked at his watch for the umpteenth time, he thought that by now the man, they were holding all the traffic up for, would have been stopped. Two hours of frustration by both the Police and the traffic drivers, had resulted in nothing happening. He decided to call Gray and see if there was any further news from the Station. Stepping onto the pavement, he radioed in and after a few minutes was put through to Gray.

"Well?" asked Gray.

"No sign of him or his car."

"We must have missed him then. Close it up, and come back in. I think we need to take a new look at that Inn in Brora, The Harbour Inn, I mean. Bill and Jane reported seeing the man coming and going from there, before he drove off South, now he may or may not have left something there, but I think we should take a second look. Meet me there in, say fifteen minutes." Gray hung up. Cooper looked at the traffic, now queuing down main street, sighing indicated to the other officers, to open up the road. They quickly moved the barriers out of the way, and the traffic, slowly started to move North and South, it would be a short while before it flowed normally, Cooper thought to himself, but he went and got into his car, and started up the blue lights, cars and lorries parted like the red sea before him as he drove along the A9 towards Brora.

+

Gray swung his car into the small road before the bridge and drove along under the bridge pulling up at The Harbour Inn. Cooper was already parked and waiting outside the front of the Inn.

"Side door is pulled shut, but not locked Sir."

"That's where Bill said he saw the man coming out from the Inn." The two men moved around the side and pushed the door carefully open, not a sound greeted them. Cooper, taking the lead, moved in first. Walking quickly through the storeroom and into the Bar area, behind the bar. He pointed at the pump signs.

"Still lit, the electric must be on."

"Better be careful though, especially if somebody has already been here." Gray flashed his torch down onto the floor, were a set of footprints in the light dust could be clearly seen.

"Maybe we should call in forensics, you know how touchy they can be if we have walked through a potential crime scene." Said Cooper.

"Find the light switch and let's have some real light on." Cooper flashed his torch around near the door and saw a bank of six switches, he switched them all on and went to join Gray, who was now at the bar, looking over the counter.

"See anything important Sir?"

"Yes, no cheese and onion crisps, pity I fancied some. Look at the mirror hanging behind the bar, funny angle wouldn't you say?" Gray pointed his finger at a mirror that ran the total length of the bar above the optics and spare glasses, as Gray had said, it was slightly at an angle. By looking carefully, they both could see the trapdoor had been left open in the floor area.

"Why do you think the mirror is angled then Cooper?" asked Gray.

"So, he can see the customers as he comes up from the cellar, make sure nobody is helping themselves, to crisps and like." He added sarcastically.

"Right, but we passed the shelves of bottled beer and other drinks as we came in. So, what else would be down there?"

"Beer barrels?"

"Getting warm, now let's call in the forensics and wait, as you said they don't like us trampling all over the place."The two men retreated back out of the Inn and radioed in that a forensic team was needed and quickly. As the two policemen waited, Cooper's radio made a noise. Acknowledging it, Cooper pressed the button and spoke.

""DS Cooper."

"Forensic will not be with you tonight, a body has been discovered in Dornoch, a burglary was called in and when we got there, a body was found on the floor of the flat. You are to lock up and get over to Dornoch, Dornoch Police are controlling the scene, but if it linked to your case, then they will hand it over."

"Copy that, go to Dornoch after locking up Inn."

"Yes." Cooper went over Gray, who was sat looking at the paper lying on the table. He related the message, Gray looked up and stood up quickly.

"Come on then, get this locked up, and seal it as well. That might stop anybody trying to get back into the Inn." He led the way back through the passage and out to the clear cold afternoon air. Cooper pulled the door closed and using a plastic police tie, secured the handle. He noted reference number on the tie, now the only way in was through the front door, so he went and did the same there before joining Gray.

"All secure."

"Let's go to Dornoch."The two men moved to their cars, turned in the road before putting the blue lights on and the siren sounding through the silent harbour. In his room at the hotel, Patrick watched them go, before getting his recently bought torch and putting on his waterproof jacket, he left the hotel, this time walking down the road, and under the railway bridge before walking up to the Inn. He went first to the main door, then seeing the plastic tie, cursed quietly. He moved to the side entrance, that was secured in a similar fashion. So, the police thought the place sealed did they? He walked down to the front of the harbour and along towards the old icehouse, long since abandoned, but he had found a passageway, some years earlier, that went from the Inn to the icehouse. He had assumed it had been built to avoid taking ice out into the sunshine, if there was any sun in this part of the world, he thought ruefully. A simple change of padlock, the old one being cut off, before a new combination lock had replaced it. Turning at the doors to the old icehouse, he spun the numbers to the chosen four digits. The padlock clicked open and he stepped inside before pulling the door closed and relocking the padlock behind him. He switched on his torch, made his way towards the back of the building, where a pile of lobster pots stood piled in front of the wall. He quickly moved them to one side revealing a metal studded door set into the stone wall. He pushed the handle down, pulling at the same time. The door swung silently open a light came on as it did so. Patrick turned his torch off and walked forward down the corridor which went under the road between the Icehouse and the Inn. Once in the Inn's cellar, he put his torch back on and shone it around the room, rows of casks of beer stood on the floor, the plastic pipes going up to the bar above. Not all of the casks had beer in them. Some were empty. Quickly he moved the empty ones away, revealing a row of shelves, each shelf had blocks of Cocaine sitting on them, a fortune if the police had found them, but at the moment they were still there, waiting for the next boat to collect them. Taking four at a time, two in each hand he set off down the corridor moving them to the Icehouse.

Two hours later, he was half done. Deciding to stop and return the next day, he went back out the way he had come, carefully closing the doors behind him, all he had left, if he had looked, was the outlines of the blocks on the shelves, where the dust hadn't settled. Nor had he replaced the empty casks in front of the shelves. An hour later, having returned to the hotel. Patrick was sat in the window of the hotel, looking through the binoculars at the Inn, in case anything or anybody should show up.

CHAPTER 44

Gray and Cooper had taken over the case. Much to the relief of the local Inspector. Everybody on the team were encased in protective clothes, to avoid any contamination of the scene. The Doctor had been and pronounced the person dead, dead through strangulation, he had added, about five days ago, before leaving them to it, Gray turned to the Cooper.

"Notice anything?"

"No flies?"

"Exactly, no flies after five days. The place should be swarming with them, but nothing. Somebody has been here before us." He turned to the lead forensic person. "See if there are any signs of anybody being in the flat since the death of the lady here?." Having said that, both men stepped outside the flat. Gray nodded towards the flat. "Has to be a theft of some kind or otherwise why kill her? There are thousands of pounds of antiques in there, yet none taken. Why?"

"Hard to dispose of perhaps? Maybe it's cash that was stolen?"

"Maybe once they have finished, we can take a good look."

"In the meantime, I don't know about you, but I am starving. Food has to be available somewhere near here." Said Cooper looking at Gray.

"There is, the Nosebag, it's on Castle Street." Gray led them down the stairs and towards Castle St, where sure enough, a sign hung of a donkey eating out of a bag. The two men entered and ordered some food.

+

The Stubbs had sold, at least the man said he was coming back with the rest of the money. Feeling a bit guilty towards the lady who had sold it to her, as it was going for a lot more than she had first thought. Deciding to share the good news, she dialled the phone number the lady had given her and waited for her to answer and get the good news.

+

In Dornoch, the phone rang in the flat and although forensics tried to ignore it, it rang on and on. Fed up with it ringing, a member of the team picked up the receiver.

"Hello, is that Ms Saunders, I've sold the Stubbs, and thought.."

"Excuse me, I am not Ms Saunders, who are you, you are talking to the police and we are investigating a crime. What cheque stubs are you talking about?"

"Not cheque stubs, Stubbs, the Painter, I've sold it for you, her I mean. I had given her money for it, as a cheque and cash, and sold it for a lot more than I thought I would get for it. I wanted to tell her that I'll send up the rest as soon as the money clears."

"Let's get this right, you have sold a painting that the owner of this flat asked you to sell for her?"

"Yes!"

"And you are phoning from where exactly?"

"Oxford. Oxford High Antiques."

"Right.. Well, Oxford High Antiques, it looks as though the lady will not be able to talk to you today, but somebody will contact you soon. In the meantime, keep hold of the paperwork and money." He hung up and returned to his work, dusting the wooden handle of the settee, where a nice thumb print was showing. He took a photo and then captured the print using the usual techniques, before moving on to the other end of the settee, where a second hand had obviously been held. He repeated the exercise and then progressed through the other items of furniture. He forgot all about the phone call from Oxford..

+

Gray, seated in his car, watched the flat, the first of the team had come out on to the steps and had left about ten minutes ago, now he just was waiting for last one to leave, then they could get the flat to themselves.

+

Two hours later, a frustrated Gray and Cooper had found nothing of any interest in the flat, the outline of where a picture on the wall should have been, had not gone unnoticed by Gray. Nothing else seemed to be missing. They didn't even know the name of the owner, or if that was the person who was found dead in the flat. One thing of note had been a piece of paper with a scribbled Oxford number on it, Cooper had bagged and tagged it, and it now was in Coopers jacket pocket as they drove in their respective cars back to Golspie. Once back at their desks, Cooper pulled the large file of paperwork towards him, he recalled something about an Oxford phone number cropping up before this one. He found it, a few minutes later, the same number as on the paper they had found in the house next door. He went out and found the original and compared the two evidence bags, definitely the same number.

Going back to his desk, he sat down and dialled it. After a few minutes it was still ringing. He hung up and then dialled his contact with BT to see if they had got any further in tracing the number from when they had found the first piece of paper with the number on.

+

Patrick had been watching The Harbour Inn intently and had jumped when his mobile had rung, he glanced at the screen, it was showing that it was a forwarded number from his Oxford landline. Ignoring it, he carried on watching the doors of the Inn.

+

Cooper walked through to Gray and showed him the two pieces of paper with the same number and explained that he had tried phoning but still no answer, but BT were getting back to him later to say whereabouts in Oxford it might be.

Bill and Jane were packing, the holiday, if you could call it that, was over, time to get back to work, London beckoned. The last few items were crammed into a plastic bag, before Jane picked it up, along with her handbag and took a last look around the room. Bill had already gone down to the car on two occasions now he stood with one small bag over his shoulder,

"What do you think happened here all those years ago, Bill?"

"I don't know, probably never will, we have bigger things to think about down south, I doubt we will hear or have to return back here again. Although I still think the cases are connected in some way."

"Spoken as though you were working the case. You are on holiday, remember them?" She lightly punched him on the arm. "I suppose we should tell Gray that we are leaving the area."

"Probably." He picked up the key to the room, placing it with his own, they walked down to the reception area. Bill rang the bell, the lady behind the counter looked up.

"We are checking out, here are the keys to our room, can we have our bill please?"

"Certainly, what name is it, with all the staff problems, I am still trying to find my way around things."

"Mr and Mrs Dawson. Old Poultney was the suite."

"Ah yes, here we are." She took a piece of paper out of a pigeonhole and passed it to him. "This was left today for you." She bent over her computer and typed in some details, a few minutes later the printer under the counter came to life and printed out two copies of the invoice. Sweeping them up together, she passed them over to Bill to check that everything was alright. He ran his eyes over the totals, nothing seemed out of the ordinary, so gave her his credit card to charge it to. She looked at the card and then up at Bill. "The name is not Dawson on the card."

"No, we are here undercover, so to speak, that is my real name. Look I'll sign this piece of paper, you can compare signatures." Suiting the action to the word, he did so, and slid the paper across for her to compare.

"Right you are, she phoned the card through for authorisation, and having got that, stamped the invoice 'PAID' before passing it over to him. "I do hope the events that have happened haven't put you off returning again someday." She said as he put the invoice into his jacket pocket.

"Not really, but it is a bit far to come from London."

"Quite so, I do understand. Well, goodbye then." With that she turned and went back into the office, Jane and Bill left the hotel and walked down to the car. As Bill started the engine, he looked at Jane.

"We'll call in and tell Gray and Cooper we are leaving then?"

"Better do so. It will make things easier, later on, I mean." They drove out down the drive, Bill giving a glance at the Broch for the last time.

+

At the police station BT had got back to Cooper, who now had been told that the closest they could get to identifying the number was in the location of Headington or possibly Marston, somewhere between those two areas anyhow. Cooper went through to Gray and broke the news. At the front desk, Bill and Jane were asking to see them both.

+

"What do you mean, you are going back to London?" We haven't said you can leave. You stayed here twenty-five years ago, seem to know a lot of what is going on. I need you to stay." Said Gray. Jane looked across at Bill as if to say, 'I told you this would happen'.

"The thing is, we have work to do in London, this was not supposed to be work, if there was anything we could do to help, then we would, but there isn't is there?" asked Bill.

"Ok, suppose I tell you as much as I know, see if that changes your mind. I do ask that you keep this to yourselves though."

"Oh, don't worry about that, we have signed the official secrets Act, haven't we Jane?"

"Yes." She smiled sweetly at Gray and Cooper. "So, tell all."

"Well in no particular order, we have the following happening in what was a sleepy part of Sutherland. One, a body found in an attic of a hotel and two people die in same hotel twenty five years earlier. Two, a body is found in a flat in Dornoch, Three, a manager and receptionist leave the hotel in a hurry, and one gets killed and the other goes off who knows where? Four, an Inn in Brora is suddenly closed, soon after opening and a boat vanishes, a boat that only you two have seen, but did manage to photograph. Five, a picture, though what of, has been taken from the flat in Dornoch. Six, a kilo of cocaine is found next door to this police station. Seven, a phone number is found in the flat in Dornoch and in the house next door. So, any ideas at all?" He pleaded with them.

"Sounds like drugs to me. I'd concentrate on that angle for now. You forgot the two men fighting in the Broch back in the fifties." Said Bill with a smile. "Chase the money, that will probably lead you in the right direction. You might hear from us again someday." He put out his hand for Gray to shake. Gray responded, then looked at them both.

"You never have said who you work for?"

"Government Department." Replied Jane with a straight face.

"Both of us." Said Bill. "We really must be going, it's been nice meeting with you, I hope, we hope, you crack the case soon." They turned and left his office and walked out to the car parked in the carpark opposite the Police station. Once on their way, Jane looked at Bill and laughed. He will be furious when he finds out, you know."

"I know, but what could I do. You know that we both know the links are to Oxford and Amsterdam and possibly London. Nobody gave Golspie or Brora a thought as it being a passing place for smuggling drugs into the UK. The ports are all looked at, as are the airports and the channel tunnel, but not the small coastal villages like these."

"We had better talk to London, fill them in on what is going on up here, if Gray hasn't done so already." Said Jane. "Do we go into Dornoch, take a look around at the flat? Or what about the phone number, I noticed you didn't give that back to Gray when he showed you it. Where is it by the way?"

"In my outer jacket pocket, the left hand one. Fish it out, and phone the number to the office, they will get the person a lot quicker than BT." Bill said with a laugh.

CHAPTER 45

Patrick, 'The Boss' arrived back in Oxford. He was cross and upset, what should have been a routine transfer of drugs, had ended with all of it being lost to the Police. The Amsterdam end of the operation were not at all happy, understandable when you realised that the total value of the two tons was in the region of Twenty six thousand pounds at wholesale price. Cut and refined, the value grew exponentially. He was made even more upset, to find that 'The Stubbs' had been sold. To a rich Oxford person was all he had been told. Word had gone out on the street that he would pay good money to find the buyer, also, to find out anything about the location of Eva, though he thought it un-likely that she would be found. Somebody could choose to disappear easily, as he knew only too well. In the meantime, he needed to find a new base to bring the stuff in from abroad, Scotland had been chosen as being considered so far away that nobody would take any notice. The cost of the Scottish side had been large, an Inn that couldn't be used again, a cottage ditto, a boat that would need a major repaint and change of shape to avoid being seen and recognised as well as the drugs themselves. The phone rang on his desk, a new number had been selected, after the old one seemed to be having problems connecting to his mobile for some reason.

"Yes?"

"The Boss?"

"Yes. Who is this?"

"Listen carefully, Ronald Burgess bought the Stubbs. Here is his address. The Tall Pine, Old Headington, Oxford. He has a habit of killing people, to the best of our knowledge, he has killed two people who he didn't get to fall in with him. It may be more, be careful if you see him." The phone went dead. He leaned back and selected a cigar from his humidifier and cut the end off, before phoning one of his henchmen to arrange a visit to Mr Burgess, who would be invited to come and discuss donating to his favourite charity.

+

Thomas Swift put the phone down and looked at Bill and Jane. They had used their department staff to trace all the visitors of the hotel. He had been seen in Dornoch and Golspie and then had vanished. A lot of phone calls had resulted in finding him and persuading him to come on the side of the Angels. His phone call, they hoped, would lead to the capture of the man that they knew of as 'The Boss'. Ronald had been too friendly with Thomas, so after Thomas had left the flat, he had waited until he saw Ronald leave, then he had returned and seen through the window the body on the floor. He had got as far away from Dornoch as fast as he could. He had made it to Oxford, not realising that he was putting himself closer to the centre of things.

"Do you think he'll go to Ronald?" He asked.

"I think so, the picture alone he wants for some reason, the owner of the shop selling it, has noticed the same faces on the high street for a number of weeks now. The Police getting the cocaine in Brora will have probably hurt him badly. As well as those contacts who supply it to him."

"Did you ever identify the lady?" Asked Thomas in a casual manner.

"Diane, oh yes, Diane Saunders, or alias Bird or Mitchell. She was a runner of drugs in Oxford in the sixties, but had the misfortune to get her drug money, well not hers exactly, stolen after taking her final exams. A bright lady, made a name for herself, blackmailing men after sleeping with them, small but regular amounts, then she disappeared for a number of years. Seems she was in Dornoch." Said Jane. She turned towards Bill. "Did you tell Gray about the thumb print on the settee?" Bill looked sheepish.

"Nope. I'll phone him now." He picked up his phone and asked to be connected to Golspie Police Station, a DI Gray. A few minutes later he was on the line.

"Good to hear from you Bill. Any news?"

"Well yes, a couple of things, one is there is a development down here, a Mr Burgess is your suspect for the death of the woman in Dornoch, she was called Diane Saunders, Bird or Mitchell, went under all three names or aliases. The second is that there was a thumbprint on the wooden part of the settee, identified as belonging to a Mr Ronald Burgess."

"Hang on a minute, how would you know all that?"

"Sorry to do this to you, we both work in the London based at the International Crime Department. We had a sniff that the East side of Sutherland might be fertile ground so to speak." Gray tapped furiously at his computer as they talked, he was trying to find their names on the internal police computer programme.

""Don't believe you, you aren't on the list of people working down there."

"Well be that as it may, Mr Burgess is being tracked in Oxford and we think it might lead us to the main man, nobody knows his name, other than he is known as 'Mr Big' don't ask me why, have never seen a photo or a description of the man." Bill hung up and turned to Jane.

"He doesn't believe us."

"Well he will do, once the news breaks."

+

Ronald sat in his office, he had the picture hung over the fireplace. As agreed he had settled up with the owner. He didn't give a second thought to the murders in East Sutherland, he had become immune to them. The front doorbell rang, he ignored it, they would go away if he didn't answer it. It rang again, and again. Annoyed now, he got up and walked to the front door. As soon as he opened it, two men dressed from head to toe in black, one carrying a sawn off double barrelled shotgun, came into the house and pushed him through and down into a kitchen chair. He started to speak but got a fist in the face for his trouble. The second man had, meantime, tied his ankles and wrists to the chair with plastic ties. The first one looked at him.

"Ronald Burgess?"

"Yes, but there is some mistake you know, you must believe me."

"Don't know about that, our boss, well 'The Boss' wants a word with you. So, you had better come and listen to what he has to say."

"I can't go anywhere tied like this." He struggled against the ties, but to no avail. The two men looked at one another, laughed and picked up the chair, with him still attached and took it out to the white van parked outside. Once there, the first returned and took the painting off the wall, before returning to the van.

+

Twenty minutes later, two unmarked police cars turned into the drive and parked and started to watch his house.

CHAPTER 46

A month later...

The Police had thoroughly searched The Harbour Inn, and had found half of the cocaine, they also had found the passageway to the icehouse, but had left it where it was, while keeping a watch on it from the other side of the river. They hoped that somebody would come and collect the remaining cocaine when they could swoop and catch them red handed. So far, nothing had happened.

DI Gray sat at his desk, writing up a report on what had led to the seizure of one of the biggest hauls of cocaine to be found in Scotland.

+

A man had been found dead, and tied to a kitchen chair, what dental work remained in his mouth, after a shot had been fired through it, as well as his remaining finger, had confirmed it was a man known as Ronald Burgess. A frame of a painting had been found around his neck.

+

Thomas Swift moved to Headington and bought a house cheaply which nobody else wanted to buy, a nice house in Old Headington, he thought he had a bargain.

+

Eva settled to the life of a bookseller, eventually ending up as Assistant Manager. She arranged for full UK Citizenship after five years of working in London.

+

'The Boss' moved from Oxford, but to where, nobody knows, he is still being hunted both in the UK and Europe. Cocaine supplies dipped for a few months but are starting to climb back up.

Bill and Jane continue to work for the London and International Crime Department.

Two Months later...

DI Gray sat at his desk looking at a large A4 envelope, a thick one that had come internally from London.

"Dear Inspector Gray, we feel that you should be told about the case we were working on, we've written out in note form, which you will find in the enclosed. For obvious reasons, we were unable to stay in your part of the world under our real names, so used aliases. If you need to ever contact us again, write to us at The London and International Crime Department… Thanks for your understanding and assistance.

Signed

W & J Sutherland

Now read the first chapter in No Body at Ben Bhraggie.

NO BODY AT BEN BHRAGGIE

A DI Sutherland Case

Chapter 1

Golspie 1992 Late Summer.

She raced through the trees, stumbling on tree roots. She could hear the pursuers back behind her. Breathless, she knew if she stopped that would be the end of her. Onwards up through the dark woods. She had a lamp strapped to her headband, but dare not switch it on. They would see her at once. A new sound came into the night, the sound of a helicopter. Wondering if it was looking for her or another person she raced onwards. Her heart pounded as she crossed the wide track used by the logging lorries. Snatching a rare glance behind her, she could see lights off torches flashing in-between the trees. Grabbing a quick lungful of air, she fingered the pendent around her neck. Then bent down and raced onwards, her foot nearly going into a rabbit hole on the track. Voices were now being heard calling out for her to stop. Ignoring them, she raced onwards up the scree towards the top of the monument. Once there, she would be safe or so she had been told. A door in the base of the statue was access to a safe place to be in the event of a sudden storm or descending fog. As if being chased wasn't enough, there was a roll of thunder followed shortly by a large flash of lightening. Then the rain started, slowly at first, then becoming heavier. The ground that had been nice and firm, now started to have trickles of water running down the pathway. A lightening flash lit up the area. She saw she was now just a few yards from the top. The helicopter swooped low, skimming over her head. She felt her foot slide in the track and instinctively put out her hand to grab something, anything. The stones slide out of her hand and she fell. A shot rang out, but missed her. Now bent almost double, she started back up towards the monument. Ten more yards and she would be safe, she told herself. Torches were now picking her out against the outline of the hill. Even bent down, there was no cover. She knew that she only had a few minutes left. Reaching the brick base, she saw there was no door on that side, so staggered around the base looking for the promised door. After covering three of the sides it only left the one on the steepest side. She peered round nervously. There was no door there either. Swearing, she stretched out her fingers to clutch the brickwork, trying to grab a hold of something, anything, but it was too late. She felt a strong hand grab her wrist and twisted it hard back on itself. Letting out a scream, she released her other hand from the brickwork, it was enough, the person behind her released their hold of her and gave a push with their other hand. She screamed as she fell lengthwise down the side, banging her head badly as she did so. Finally stopping, she fingered the pendent around her neck. With as much strength as she could muster, she tore it off then swallowed it. A flash of lightening lit up the night sky and she heard and then felt a bullet pierce her arm. Half dazed, she looked at her arm where blood was coming out in spurts and gave her last groan.

Two men, coming up behind the gunman, looked down on the body sprawled across the side of the hill.

"One of us will need to go and retrieve the item. We dare not go back without it."

"Have you seen how steep that side is?"

"Yes, but it needs to be done."

"Agreed, but let's return in the morning at dawn. There will be enough light then and we can bring some ropes."

"What if anybody sees her or finds it?"

"I doubt that anybody in their right mind will be out tonight, not even in Golspie. Certainly not up here in a thunderstorm. Come on, it's getting heavier." The rain had certainly increased in the last hour. They gradually made their way back down to the village.

+

The next day, at dawn, saw a Maria and Emma, a pair of local runners, set out to carry out their normal early morning run from the centre of Lady Sutherland Road up to the top of Ben Bhraggie. They ran steadily and without using too much breath. Soon they had got into their regular pace. An hour later they had both reached the top and were looking out to sea. The older one glanced down and saw the body sprawled out on the side.

"Here, come and take a look. There is a body down there." He pointed to the spot as the other runner came over and looked down where he pointed.

"They will be soaked. I'll go down and see if they are ok."

"Really? If they were alive, they probably would be moving or waving their hands. No, they are dead. We need to head back to Golspie and report this to the police. Come on."Turning away from the body, they both set off at a faster pace by going down the back of the hill, longer but easier than running through the trees.

+

The three men appeared through the trees and made their way up towards the top. Tired and annoyed that they had had to make a return trip. The fact that it was now later than they had planned didn't improve their tempers either. They had made no sound as they climbed the last few yards. Taking a rope that they had brought with them, they tied it around the base of the monument, then throw it out and down to where the body lay.

Two hours later, a search of the area near the body had not found the pendent. Giving up and taking the body with them, they had vanished back into the trees.

+

A Police Land Rover, it's blue lights flashing, drove up the track around the back of the hill, inside the two runners and two policemen were being driven back to recover the body. The vehicle approached the top and made its way carefully to the monument. Parking alongside it, they all got out. The wind whipping their jackets.

"The body is on the South side, halfway down." Shouted one of the runners.

"Ok, we'll unwind the winch and go down. You stay in the vehicle." He turned back and throw a switch on the dashboard, at once there was a whine as the winch motor started. The other policeman had got out and made his way over to the south side. Holding on to the edge of the base, he peered around and down. Nothing there. Looking to both the right and the left, he saw nothing at all. He stepped back and beckoned at the other policeman. The man stepped out of the Land Rover and made his way over to his colleague.

"What is it?" He shouted above the noise of the wind.

"Nothing there, take a look." He stepped back to let his colleague see for himself.

"What the ?" He exclaimed as he looked down. He turned back and they both made their way back to the shelter of the Land Rover. Once inside they turned to the two runners.

"Nothing there. If you have been wasting our time.." He left the sentence unfinished.

"Nothing there? There was a body there this morning at dawn. We both saw it."

"Maybe she wasn't dead after all, maybe she was concussed and came around before making her way down by herself." Suggested the other policeman.

"She wasn't moving, not that we could see from the top that is."

"Well nobody is there now. So, this is what we are going to do. We are going back to the station and suggest you go home and tell nobody about this episode. Agreed?"

"But."

"No buts, if you say nothing then we don't have to do a lot of paperwork about nothing. If you get my drift?" He turned and started the car, remembering to wind the winch back in before setting off down to the village.

+

Once back in the village, the two runners made their way to their respective houses. Both were fuming that the police had not believed them. Yet both knew what they had seen that morning was real enough.

+

The phone rang on the desk. His current flunky picked it up and listened before handing it to The Boss, with a smile on his face.

"Yes?"

"We've got the body, but not the pendent."

"Did you look for it?"

"Yes, but no sign of it. It is rather small to see."

"I know that, but it is essential for my safety. Have you disposed of the body yet?"

"Not yet."

"Get to it, put it somewhere where nobody will see it for a couple of weeks, but where animals might feed for free, if you get my drift?"

"Got you." The line went dead. The Boss lent back in his chair and looked across at the man stood by his desk.

"Do the Russians know that the pendent is missing? He asked the man. Without saying a word, the man shook his head. He knew better than to answer back a rhetorical question. He had witnessed what had happened to his predecessor who had done that. Not very pleasant for anybody to see. The Boss leaned back in his chair before standing and walking over to the window and looking out at the passing boats on the Thames.

"Any other calls or.." The Boss left the sentence hanging. But his flunky knew what he meant. Had the Dutchman been in touch.

"No, I haven't heard from the Dutchman, not this week anyhow."The Boss took out a cigar and cut the end off, before striking a match, lighting it and puffing gently to get it going. He flung the spent match out of the open window.

"Maybe I should take a trip up to East Sutherland in the coming days. See what the lay of the land is. Check on the flat and Inn. Maybe the Dutchman could buy it and set up his own business there."The Boss shook his hand at the flunky as if to say, now get out of here. He left, leaving the Boss to his thoughts.

This is a work of fiction set in the areas of the City of Oxford and East Sutherland.

Golspie, Brora, Helmsdale, Wick, Thurso and Dornoch can all be visited and recommend doing so. Carn Liath Broch is situated halfway between Golspie and Brora and can be visited at any time. Both La Mirage & Lindsay & Co. are real businesses and well worth visiting. *The Newspapers, The Northern Times, The Oxford Mail* and *The Oxford Times* were all still in business at the time of writing.

This is a work of fiction, any similarity to any business or person, living or dead is not intentional, as all the characters, places and businesses, except those mentioned above, are drawn from the authors imagination.

As far as the author is aware there is not yet a London and International Crime Department.